The Stranger in the Shadows

Nancy couldn't see Neil anywhere. If he was the blackmailer, she had to find him soon.

She searched the snow for tracks and checked the glistening ice covering the lake. It didn't look thick enough to hold a person. Nancy guessed Neil had stayed on the shore and disappeared into the trees.

Suddenly two hands shoved her hard in the back. Nancy flew forward and landed hard on the ice. Catching her breath, she pushed herself up on her hands and knees. *Crack!* The sound sent a shiver of terror through her body.

The ice was breaking beneath her!

Ice-cold water, seeping through a crack, washed over her numb fingers. She yelled for help, but the wind whisked her cry into the night sky. There was no way anyone would hear her. . . .

Nancy Drew
Mystery Stories

Available from MINSTREL Books

NANCY DREW MYSTERY STORIES®

103

NANCY DREW®

THE STRANGER IN THE SHADOWS

CAROLYN KEENE

A MINSTREL® BOOK

PUBLISHED BY POCKET BOOKS

New York   London   Toronto   Sydney   Tokyo

A MINSTREL PAPERBACK *ORIGINAL*

 A Minstrel Book published by
POCKET BOOKS, a division of Simon & Schuster Inc.
1230 Avenue of the Americas, New York, NY 10020

Copyright © 1991 by Simon & Schuster Inc.
Produced by Mega-Books of New York, Inc.

ISBN: 0-671-73049-5

First Minstrel Books printing October 1991

10 9 8 7 6 5 4 3 2 1

Cover art by Aleta Jenks

Printed in the U.S.A.

Contents

THE STRANGER
IN THE SHADOWS

1

A Clever Deception

"How do you say 'hello' in Dutch?" Nancy Drew asked her friend as they walked through the shopping mall.

"That's easy," said sixteen-year-old Suzanne Moorely. The red-haired girl stopped in front of a store window and turned to Nancy and Bess Marvin. Suzanne had been a good friend of Bess's since junior high.

"*Hallo!*" Suzanne said. "When my mom and I found out our exchange student would be from the Netherlands, that's the first thing we learned how to say. And *goedendag* means 'good day' or 'good-bye.'"

Nancy repeated the words, then laughed. "Boy, did I mess that up."

"No, that was good," Suzanne insisted. "Paula will think it's great if you greet her in Dutch."

"Let me try," Bess said, then repeated the Dutch words.

Nancy and Suzanne burst out laughing.

Bess giggled, too. "Okay, okay, so I flunked foreign languages."

The three girls continued strolling through the crowded River Heights Mall. They were on their way to meet Paula de Jagger, the exchange student who was living with Suzanne and her family.

"Paula's been here since August," Suzanne told Nancy and Bess. "Only five months in the States and already she speaks perfect English. In fact," Suzanne added with a sigh, "everything she does is perfect."

"So how did she get a job at Around the World?" Nancy asked. "I hear it's a really neat boutique."

"She's not really working," Suzanne explained. "Foreign exchange students can't get paying jobs, so Paula volunteers. She wants to open her own shop in the Netherlands someday."

"It sounds like a dream come true," Bess sighed. "All the amazing clothes and fantastic jewelry—I'd be in heaven."

"Paula is, too. Except . . ." Suzanne's voice trailed off.

"Except what?" Nancy prompted.

"Well, lately she's been acting a little strangely."

"What do you mean?" Nancy asked as they walked past a fountain and stepped onto an escalator.

"It's hard to say." Suzanne frowned and bit her

2

lip. "It's like, one day she's happy and the next day she's depressed. No one else in my family seems to notice, though, so maybe I'm crazy."

Bess raised her eyebrows. "Maybe Paula's moping over a guy."

"Or maybe she's homesick," Nancy suggested.

"Maybe." Suzanne's voice sounded doubtful.

When the girls got off the escalator on the second floor, Suzanne put her hand on Nancy's arm. "Listen, after you meet Paula, will you watch her and see if you notice anything?"

Nancy shrugged. "Sure."

"Wow!" Bess halted in front of the window of Glad Rags, a trendy women's clothing store. "Look at that great outfit."

Nancy laughed. "Bess, since we've been here, you've seen at least twelve great outfits. Though I must admit, that is cute." Nancy cocked her reddish-blond head to admire the dark blue knit sweater and skirt.

"Those stretchy outfits show every extra pound," Suzanne said, glancing at her own clothes. Like Nancy, she was dressed casually in jeans and a sweater. Nancy was tall and slender, and Suzanne was an inch shorter and muscular.

"That's for sure," Bess said, grimacing. "I'd have to go on a serious diet before I wore anything that tight." Bess was hiding the five extra pounds she wanted to lose under a long bulky blue top that matched the color of her eyes. A gold barrette kept her long blond hair away from her face. All three girls had boots on, and their winter coats were slung over their arms. The weather forecaster had predicted snow.

"Well, we'd better get going." Suzanne tugged at Bess, who was inching toward the store's entrance and a rack of colorful dresses. "Paula read in the paper about the last case you solved, Nancy. She really wants to meet the 'famous teen detective.' We can surprise her."

"You mean she doesn't know we're coming?" Bess asked.

Suzanne shook her head. "I couldn't pin her down on a day, so I thought we'd just show up and maybe take her to dinner or something. She's so popular we barely get a chance to talk."

Nancy thought she heard a trace of bitterness in Suzanne's voice. Was the redheaded girl jealous of Paula?

Suzanne pointed across the walkway. "There's the store. It just opened a month ago. Paula says business is booming. They have clothes, accessories, and jewelry from all over the world."

The three girls headed toward the boutique. Above the entrance, the words Around the World were written in fancy gold script.

Nancy paused to admire the window display. A green-haired mannequin was dressed in a skin-tight, gold-sequined gown. Next to it stood a life-size china leopard draped with emerald necklaces. In the background hung brightly colored parrots made of papier-mâché and feathers.

4

"What a wild display," Nancy said. "It really catches your eye."

"Paula designed it, of course," Suzanne said, rolling her eyes.

There was no doubt about it, Nancy thought. Suzanne was jealous of the exchange student.

"Wow, Paula's really talented," Bess said.

"You don't have to tell *me*," Suzanne said. "Miss Paula Perfect has a list ten miles long of all the things she can do."

"Do I detect a little jealousy?" Bess teased her friend.

Suzanne shrugged. "Maybe. But why not? Paula even made the cheerleading squad. Can you believe it? I've tried out three years in a row and never even gotten called back. Then there are her grades." She groaned. "If my parents tell me, 'Gee, Suzanne, if only you could get all A's like Paula,' one more time, I'll run away from home. Sometimes I think things sure would be a lot easier if Paula went back to the Netherlands early."

"Oh, you don't really mean that," Nancy said. Then she stopped. "Hey, look at that picture frame. Come on, you guys," she said, starting into the store. "It would make a great birthday present for George." George Fayne was Bess's cousin, who was away on a skiing trip.

Suzanne caught up to Nancy. "Don't forget about watching Paula," she said in a low voice.

Nancy nodded, but she couldn't help wondering why Suzanne was being so dramatic.

5

"Hi!" a friendly voice greeted them. A tall, willowy girl waved from the middle of the crowded store. Her white-blond hair hung down her back in a French braid, and her blue eyes sparkled as she came toward the three girls.

Nancy could see one reason why Suzanne might be jealous. Dressed in a short leather skirt, ankle-high boots, and silky blouse, Paula looked like a fashion model.

"Hi, Paula," Suzanne said. "Come meet my friends Nancy and Bess."

"Hallo, Paula," Nancy said, remembering her Dutch hello. "I'm Nancy."

Paula's face broke into a big grin. "And I'm glad to meet the famous detective. Suzanne has told me all about some of the cases you've had to solve. It sounds so exciting."

"And I'm Bess, the famous detective's friend," Bess chimed in.

"Oh, yes, and I've heard a lot about you, too," Paula added.

"We've come to take you to dinner," Suzanne said.

"Dinner?" Paula's smile faltered. "Well, that would be nice, but could you come back later? Things have been so busy this evening—"

"Wow, look at that necklace!" Bess's enthusiastic gasp cut Paula short. She walked over to a glass-enclosed display case filled with turquoise and silver jewelry from the Southwest.

Nancy joined her. The sparkling necklaces,

6

rings, and bracelets were spread across a striped Indian blanket. A tomahawk, arrowhead, and several ceramic pots were arranged behind them.

"Where did the store get the pottery and artifacts?" Nancy asked. "They look real."

Paula nodded. "They are. Since I didn't know that much about American Indians, I went to check out some books at the library. Luckily for me, they had this stuff from an exhibit and were happy to lend it out."

"You mean you arranged this?" Bess asked, sounding impressed.

"That's right." Paula checked her watch and glanced toward the front of the boutique. "Why don't I meet you all somewhere? I usually get a dinner break about now, but it's been so jammed, I'm not sure when I can get off. Only the manager, Ms. Hunt, and I are working tonight." She gestured at a stylishly dressed older woman ringing up a sale at the cash register.

"That sounds fine to me." Nancy looked around for Suzanne. The redheaded girl was hanging back, fingering some embroidered vests. Nancy wondered why Suzanne had asked her to watch Paula closely. As far as she could tell, there wasn't one thing unusual about Paula de Jagger. The exchange student was vivacious, talented, and obviously cared about her job. Maybe Suzanne was inventing things, hoping to make Paula seem a little less "perfect."

7

"What would you like to eat?" Nancy asked Suzanne.

"How about pizza?" Bess suggested. "We can go over to the Pizza Palace and order."

"Maybe we should let Paula choose," Nancy said, turning to the exchange student.

"Oh, I think—" Paula began, then stopped abruptly. Frowning, she gazed over Nancy's shoulder.

Nancy turned. All she saw was Ms. Hunt, waiting on another customer.

"We could go to the Eateries," Bess said. "That way, we can get a whole bunch of different things and share them."

"Sounds good to me," Suzanne agreed. "How about it, Paula?"

But Paula was still staring off into space.

"Paula?" Suzanne looked intently at the girl.

"Huh?" The tall blonde's head whirled around.

"Are the Eateries okay?" Suzanne asked.

"Sure, that would be fun," Paula said quickly. "I'll meet you there." Plastering a smile on her face, she began to herd the girls toward the entrance.

"Excuse me," she said. "I have to help someone."

After Paula left, Suzanne clutched Nancy's arm. "See what I mean?" she whispered. "One minute she's friendly, and the next it's like she's in outer space."

"Well, the boutique *is* busy, I guess," Nancy said.

"Hey, guys," someone called from behind a shelf.

8

"Check these out." Bess peered around a giant stuffed unicorn, and Nancy and Suzanne walked back into the store to join her. Bess held up two dangly earrings made of shells. "Great, huh?"

But when she saw Suzanne's frown, Bess set the earrings down. "I thought they were kind of neat," she said with a shrug.

"Suzanne's not worried about the earrings," Nancy told her friend. "She's worried about Paula."

"Something must be really bugging her," Suzanne said. "She's been like this for—"

"Stop, thief!" a voice cried loudly. Nancy whipped her head around.

"Stop!" the voice called again.

Springing into action, Nancy ran toward the cry. It was coming from near the store's entrance. She hurried around a merchandise-filled shelf, her coat and purse flying behind her.

Just inside the doorway, Paula de Jagger was struggling with a girl about her age. Paula had hold of the teenager's wrist. With her other hand, she'd grabbed the lapel of the girl's bulky coat. The girl was well dressed in leather boots and a fur-trimmed coat, and she had a stylish haircut and an expensive-looking purse.

"She's a thief," Paula told Nancy angrily.

Nancy wasn't quite sure how to react. The girl looked shocked at Paula's accusation. Had Paula actually seen her steal something?

"Let me go!" the girl shouted, trying to wrench

9

free. The sash on her coat loosened. "You can't prove anything." She glared at Paula defiantly.

"Oh, yes, I can," Paula said. Opening up the girl's coat, she reached inside and pulled out a turquoise and silver necklace. With shaking fingers, she held it up. "I think this is all the evidence the police will need."

2

Night Moves

"How'd that get in there?" the girl sputtered. She was so flustered that Nancy wasn't sure whether she was telling the truth or was just a very good actress.

"I saw you swipe this necklace from the display case," Paula replied, her voice steady. "And I bet it's not all you took." She opened the flaps of the girl's coat. Sewn into the inside lining was a pocket, and it was bulging with gold and silver jewelry.

Nancy was amazed. Paula had been right all along. The girl was obviously an experienced and clever shoplifter. Nancy was usually good at spotting someone committing a crime, but she hadn't suspected a thing.

A crowd had formed in the boutique. Over their heads, Nancy spotted a uniformed security guard striding toward them. Waving, she signaled him to hurry.

Suzanne, Bess, and Ms. Hunt were pushing their way through the crowd. "What's going on?" Ms. Hunt asked. When she saw the necklace dangling from Paula's hand, her eyes widened. "I don't believe it. I left the case unlocked for only a second."

"That was long enough," Paula said grimly.

Suddenly, the shoplifter jerked her arm from Paula's grasp. Spinning on her heels, she lunged into the crowd. Nancy reached out and grabbed her coat sleeve. At the same time, the security guard dove for the girl's wrist.

"Not so fast, kid," the guard said. "I think you have something that belongs to the store." He glanced over at Ms. Hunt. "Do you want to press charges?"

The boutique manager nodded. "I certainly do."

"I'll take her to the security office, then." The guard looked at Nancy. "Nice work."

"I wasn't the one who caught the thief." Nancy pointed to Paula. "Paula works at the store, and she saw the girl pocket the necklace."

"I'd appreciate your coming with me to fill out a report," the man told Paula.

"I'll be right down," Paula replied.

As the guard led her away, the shoplifter looked back at Paula, her eyes flashing angrily.

"We'll get you for this," she snarled.

Paula's face paled, and her fingers clutched the necklace so tightly that Nancy was afraid she'd crush the stones.

Nancy gently touched her on the shoulder. "Just

ignore her," she said quietly. "You did the right thing. She's only trying to scare you so you don't fill out that report."

The crowd began to drift away. Several people called out "good job" to Paula as they passed. The exchange student smiled uncertainly.

"Wow," Bess said. "I don't believe it. You caught a shoplifter, and we saw the whole thing. You're a real heroine."

Paula blushed and looked down at her feet. "It was nothing, really."

"Well, I never saw that girl steal the necklace," Nancy said. "I must have left my detective badge at home."

"No, really, it was nothing," Paula repeated emphatically. "I just noticed when she first came in that she seemed nervous. She kept glancing around as if to see who was watching. And she was bundled up so tight in that big coat, yet the store is quite warm." She took a deep breath. "Anyway, I'm glad it's over. Let's not talk about it anymore."

Ms. Hunt took Paula's hand and squeezed it. "Well, thank goodness you reacted as quickly as you did. Why, I unlocked the case to show a customer a ring, and the next thing I knew . . ." She shook her head. "It was all my fault."

"No, it wasn't." Paula smiled at the older woman. "It could have happened to anyone."

"You shouldn't feel bad, Ms. Hunt," Nancy added. "I'd say the shoplifter knew exactly what she was doing. I don't know how Paula spotted her. Did you ever think about becoming a detective,

Paula? You sure seem to know a lot about shoplifting."

Nancy meant the remark as a compliment, but Paula didn't seem to take it as one. Nancy wondered if the thief's angry parting words had spooked her.

"Excuse me," Paula said abruptly. "I'd better go fill out that report."

Nancy watched as she darted behind the counter and pulled out her bag and coat.

"What about dinner?" Suzanne asked as Paula passed them.

Paula didn't look up. "Uh, another time. I'm going home. I'm really tired. Nice meeting you, Nancy, Bess." Slinging her white leather bag over her shoulder, she rushed from the store.

Nancy hoped Paula wasn't going to change her mind about being a witness to the crime. Nancy knew firsthand how frightening threats could be.

Nancy watched as Paula hurried down the walkway. Just before she reached the escalator, Paula glanced nervously at a tall, dark-haired guy wearing a blue ski jacket. He tossed his soda can into the trash and started to follow her.

A coincidence, Nancy thought, frowning—or was it?

"So, is anybody else starving around here?" Bess asked.

"I am," Suzanne replied. "But I guess dinner won't be quite the same without our heroine. Now I can add 'crime fighter' to Paula's list of things she does better than me."

Nancy laughed at her friend's disgruntled expression. "Maybe a taco will help cheer you up," she said, linking her arm through Suzanne's.

"Topped off with a hot fudge sundae," Bess added, as the three girls strode from the store.

"Boy, is this pizza yummy," Suzanne said, her mouth stuffed with tomato and cheese.

The girls were seated in the plant-filled dining area that was part of the Eateries. The collection of small eating places, featuring international dishes and fast food, had just been added to the River Heights Mall.

"This place is great," Bess said. "All these tropical plants make me feel like I'm in sunny Florida. Not to mention the food!"

"Paula is missing a real feast," Nancy agreed as she speared some of Bess's tortellini.

"Yeah. I'm sorry she ducked out," Suzanne said. "But that's what I meant when I said she's been acting weird."

"Well, Paula had a good reason not to join us," Nancy reminded her. "The security officer needed her to fill out a report. I do see what you mean about her odd behavior, though."

"I thought Paula was nice," Bess said with a shrug. "So, who's ready for ice cream?"

"I am," Suzanne said, popping up. "A banana split. No, maybe a butterscotch sundae."

Nancy laughed. "I'm stuffed. You guys go ahead."

As Bess and Suzanne left to order dessert from one of the booths, Nancy began gathering up the

15

trash. She was tossing the cups, napkins, and plates into the can when she noticed Paula hurrying toward the exit opposite the Eateries. Her coat and leather bag were draped over her arm, and there was an anxious frown on her face.

Nancy wondered if Paula had had another nasty encounter with the shoplifter. Thinking back to when Paula had caught the girl stealing, Nancy recalled the threat to Paula: "We'll get you for this."

Nancy sat back down at the table. What had the girl meant by "we'll"? Had someone else been involved in the theft?

Nancy knew that shoplifters often worked in pairs. One person distracted the clerk while the other pocketed the merchandise. That probably explained it, Nancy decided. Someone else must have gotten away.

Suzanne came up to Nancy's side, licking a double-dip cone. "Want a taste?" she offered.

"No, thanks," Nancy said.

Setting her elbow on the table, Nancy rested her chin in her palm. "So tell me more about Paula."

Suzanne stopped licking her cone and sat down. "All I can tell you is that she's changed a lot. When she first came in August, she was really outgoing and friendly. She helped around the house, and we went roller-skating and shopping together."

"When did Paula start acting differently?" Nancy asked.

Suzanne thought for a moment. "I guess I noticed it in November. Paula would be her old joking self.

Then she'd get a phone call and *poof!*—like magic, she'd disappear up to her room."

"Do you have any idea who called?" Nancy asked, frowning.

Suzanne shrugged. "As far as I can tell, it was the same guy. My mom and I used to joke that Mr. Mystery was calling again."

"Hmmm," Nancy said. "And when did Paula start working at Around the World?"

"In November, too, I think." Suzanne leaned forward in her seat. "Do you think the boutique is part of the problem?" she asked eagerly.

Nancy thought Suzanne was enjoying herself too much, almost as if she *wanted* something to be wrong with Paula.

Bess joined them at the table. She was holding a giant bowl overflowing with ice cream, fudge sauce, bananas, strawberry topping, and nuts.

"Don't say anything." She shot Nancy a warning look. "I just couldn't resist the Monster Split. Besides"—she waved two spoons and grinned—"I figured you could help me eat it."

"If you insist." Laughing, Nancy took a spoon and plunked it in the gooey fudge sauce. "Anything to help a friend."

Paula de Jagger would just have to wait.

"Now that was an excellent movie," Bess said happily, a few hours later. The girls were trudging across the nearly empty parking lot of the mall. After dinner, they'd done some shopping, then gone to the ten o'clock show.

17

Soft, powdery flakes were just beginning to fall. Nancy caught one on the end of her tongue.

"I love the snow, but we'd better get home," she said as she pulled the keys to her blue sports car from her pocket. "The roads will be slippery."

The girls piled into the cold car. The engine started with a cough, then roared to life.

Nancy drove to Suzanne's house first. The Moorelys lived only a block from her own house, but she wanted a chance to talk alone with Bess.

"Maybe you guys can come over another time and get to know Paula a little better," Suzanne said as she got out of the car.

Bess and Nancy waved goodbye. As Nancy pulled out of the driveway, she turned on the wipers. The snow was falling thicker and faster.

"So what did you think?" Nancy asked.

"I think I should never have eaten all that popcorn on top of the ice cream." Bess groaned and held her stomach.

"No, I mean what did you think about Paula?"

"Well, she's beautiful and talented," Bess said. "I can see why Suzanne's a little jealous."

"Jealous enough to want Paula to go back to the Netherlands early?" Nancy pressed.

Bess gave her a funny look. "Suzanne was joking when she said that. She did seem kind of bent out of shape, but I would be, too, if I had to live with a girl who was perfect."

"Not completely perfect. Paula was acting a bit strangely," Nancy reminded her.

"Well, I didn't notice anything unusual." Bess

shrugged. "Sometimes Suzanne's a little dramatic. Besides, she's an only child and spoiled rotten." Bess chuckled. "For the first time in her life, Suzanne's not in the spotlight, and it makes her mad."

"I guess you're right," Nancy agreed. "Paula was probably just a little shaken up over the whole shoplifting incident."

"I would have been, too," Bess said. "That girl she caught was really angry."

"Mmm," Nancy said. "That reminds me. Did you see the customer Ms. Hunt was waiting on right before Paula nabbed the shoplifter?"

Bess looked puzzled. "No. But Ms. Hunt did say she'd opened the display case to show someone a necklace, so there must have been a customer. Why?"

"Well, when the thief threatened Paula, she said, 'We'll get you for this.' That started bugging me. I figured the girl had to have had an accomplice."

Bess nodded. "You think another customer got Ms. Hunt to open the jewelry case so her partner could reach in and steal the necklaces."

"Right." Nancy braked in front of Bess's house. Her friend opened the door, then turned back to Nancy.

"Maybe you'd better call the mall's security office tomorrow and tell them, just in case."

Nancy nodded. She waved to her friend, then leaned over to slam the door tight. On the floor of the car, she noticed a small shopping bag.

Nancy peeked inside the bag and saw a compact

19

disc that Suzanne had purchased at the mall. Nancy decided to drop it off on her way home.

The wipers cleared the snow off the windshield with a rhythmic swish, but Nancy still had to hunch forward to see the road. She reached the Moorelys' yellow house and pulled into the drive.

The headlights cut through the whirling snow. Nancy peered to the right of the drive. The house was dark. Suzanne must have already gone to bed.

Nancy was putting the car in reverse when a sudden movement by the garage caught her eye. A slender figure was hanging on to a tree branch that jutted over the garage. It looked as if the person was trying to climb onto the roof of the Moorelys' garage, which was attached to the house.

Quickly Nancy wiped the fogged windshield with her sleeve. Leaning forward, she peered closer. The car's high beams lit up Paula de Jagger's startled face.

Nancy's mouth fell open. What was Paula doing climbing a tree in the middle of a snowstorm?

Just then, Paula dropped onto the garage roof. But the surface was slick with new-fallen snow, and she began to slide downward.

Paula dropped to her hands and knees, but it was too late. Nancy gasped. Faster and faster, Paula slid toward the edge of the roof and the concrete drive below.

3

A Puzzling Story

Nancy cut the car engine and jumped out the door.

"Hang on, Paula!" she shouted, the wind blowing her words into the frosty air. She ran toward the double garage doors.

"Hurry!" Paula cried. Suddenly her right knee slipped out from under her. Paula screamed and clutched at the garage roof with her gloved hands. Just in time, her foot caught in the gutter and held.

Frantically, Nancy looked around for something to stand on. Then she dashed to the side door of the Moorelys' garage. She grasped the knob and turned, relieved to find it wasn't locked.

With icy fingers, Nancy flicked on the light switch. Searching the garage, she saw a stepladder propped in the corner. She quickly carried it outside and unfolded it.

A metallic screech pierced the quiet night, and Nancy looked up to see the gutter pulling away from the edge of the roof. Paula's eyes widened, and she gasped.

Nancy quickly made her way up the ladder and grabbed Paula's left ankle. "Let me guide you down," she said.

Slowly, Paula slid her left foot down the roof. For a second, it dangled in the air. Then Paula found the top step of the ladder.

"Now the right," Nancy called out.

Paula carefully shifted her weight. The gutter groaned and creaked. Nancy knew it wouldn't hold much longer.

Inch by inch, Paula drew her right foot down until it was safely on the ladder.

Nancy steadied Paula as the blond girl took one more step. Then Nancy climbed back down the ladder.

With a gasp of relief, Paula jumped into the snow beside her. "Thank you so much!" Paula gave Nancy a quick hug. "If you hadn't come along, I would be smashed on the drive."

"What were you doing up there?" Nancy asked.

Paula laughed shrilly. "Oh, it's such a silly story you wouldn't believe it. I came out to see the snow—we don't have snow storms like this in Amsterdam—and the door locked behind me."

Nancy looked puzzled. "Didn't you ring the bell?"

"I did, but no one heard." Paula shivered in the cold and wrapped her coat tighter around her. "I checked the basement and side doors, but they were locked, too. So I decided to climb up to my room." She pointed to a second-story window over-looking the garage roof.

Nancy noticed that the window was cracked open about an inch. Why would Paula leave it open in the middle of winter?

"That's kind of a steep climb," Nancy said, giving Paula a questioning look.

The exchange student laughed, but her voice sounded strained. "I guess it was a crazy idea. But I didn't realize the snow would make the roof so slippery."

"Hey! What are you guys doing down there?" Suzanne stuck her head out of an upstairs window in the front of the house.

"Playing in the snow!" Nancy joked.

"We're locked out," Paula called. "Let us in." She grabbed Nancy's icy hand. "Come on. You need to warm up with some hot chocolate."

Nancy hesitated. It had to be after midnight, but she was cold, so she decided to accept.

Paula hurried past the garage toward the front door. Nancy stopped to turn off the car lights. Then she reached into the passenger seat and picked up the bag with Suzanne's compact disc. Stuffing the bag and her frostbitten hands into her coat pockets, she followed Paula's tracks in the snow.

The tracks! If Paula *had* tried the front door earlier, why weren't there footprints in the snow? As she trudged up the snow-covered sidewalk, Nancy checked carefully. But all she could see were

23

Paula's new tracks and the faded ones Suzanne had made when Nancy dropped her off.

Had Paula tried to sneak into the house? Maybe that explained the open bedroom window and Paula's crazy explanation.

But why? Now Nancy's curiosity was aroused. As she stepped onto the front porch, she wondered what Paula was going to tell Suzanne.

The porch light flicked on, and Nancy could hear Suzanne undoing a chain lock. Next to her, Paula stamped her feet. The blond girl's hair was sprinkled with melting snowflakes, and her cheeks were flushed pink.

The front door swung open, and Suzanne peered out at them. "Are you guys crazy?" she asked as she pulled her bathrobe tightly around her. "It must be ten degrees out there."

Puffing from the cold air and stomping snow from their boots, Nancy and Paula entered the hallway. A modern chandelier cast a soft light up a spiral staircase that winded to an upstairs hall. Nancy's boots dripped snow on the hardwood floor.

The warmth felt wonderful.

Suzanne shut the door. As Nancy unbuttoned her coat, she glanced at the chain lock. To let them in, Suzanne had had to unlatch it. That meant Paula couldn't have come out the front door. The chain could not have fastened itself behind her.

"I'm the only one that's crazy," Paula laughed as she tugged off her gloves. "If my friends back home could see me now, they would be very surprised.

24

I'm always the first to get cold when we skate on the canals."

"So what were you two doing out there?" Suzanne repeated, a puzzled expression on her sleepy face.

Nancy stuck her hand in her pocket and pulled out the bag. "I stopped by to drop off your compact disc."

"Oh, thanks." Suzanne took the bag and turned back to Paula. "I thought you were home already. What's going on?"

Paula took off her coat and threw it over the banister. Nancy noticed that she was wearing the same skirt and blouse she'd had on at the mall. If Paula had been home, then gone out to look at the snow, wouldn't she have dressed in something warmer?

"Do I have to tell that silly story again?" Paula said. "No one will believe me." Grinning, Paula swung her braid over her shoulder and clapped her hands together. "But first, some hot chocolate to warm us up."

Suzanne yawned widely. "I was just about to crawl into bed."

So Suzanne hadn't been asleep yet, Nancy noted. If Paula had rung the bell, why hadn't Suzanne heard it?

Nancy followed the two girls down the hall and into the kitchen. The house was dark and silent.

"It's a good thing Mom and Dad's room is on the other side of the house," Suzanne said as she opened the cupboard door. "Otherwise, they'd be down here asking a zillion questions." She gave Paula a pointed look, but the Dutch girl ignored it.

"Just like my parents," Paula said, flashing Nancy and Suzanne her bright smile. "I think parents are the same no matter what country you live in. You should have seen my mom and dad when my brother drove my motor scooter into the canal. They were *woedend.* That's more than angry—that means furious!" She rolled her eyes and giggled.

"What happened?" Nancy asked.

"Well, Hans took my bike out before he even had his license," Paula began. She was standing in front of the stove, stirring the warm milk.

Nancy was amazed at how easily Paula had turned the conversation away from the evening's adventure. Why was she so reluctant to talk about it?

"And instead of stepping on the brake," Paula continued, "he revved up the motor and—*vroom* —it flew right into the canal."

Suzanne stopped spooning out hot chocolate mix at the table. "And since he's *your* brother, I'm sure he came out all right," she said, a tinge of sarcasm in her voice.

"Just wet and embarrassed. My parents grounded him for a month." Paula carried the saucepan of steaming milk over to the table. "But I bet Nancy's the one with good stories," she said as she poured milk into the mugs. "It must be really exciting to be a detective."

"Sometimes." Nancy stirred her hot chocolate.

"But it has its boring moments, too. I've been on stakeouts where nothing happened for hours."

"So what was your most exciting case?" Suzanne asked.

"That's hard to say." Nancy sipped her drink. "Mmm. This hits the spot."

Paula sat down opposite her. "Then what about your spookiest case?"

Nancy thought a moment. "Probably when Bess and I went to Charleston, South Carolina. We stayed in an old mansion that looked like a set for a horror movie."

"And was it haunted?" Paula asked eagerly.

"Just with greedy people." Nancy chuckled and glanced at her watch. "Wow! I didn't realize how late it was. I'd better get going, or my dad will worry."

"So soon?" Paula pouted for a moment, then brightened. "But we'll get together again. I promise I won't be working so hard the next time you come to take me for dinner."

Nancy stood up and gulped the last of her drink. "That reminds me—what happened to the shoplifter?"

Paula shook her head, yawned, and stretched. "I don't know. My, I'm tired."

Nancy set her mug in the kitchen sink. It was obvious that Paula wanted to avoid talking about the incident. Now she could understand what Suzanne had been saying at the mall. The exchange student *was* acting strange, as if she had something to hide.

Paula followed Nancy into the hall. "Thank you again for rescuing me," she whispered.

Suzanne came up behind them and peered out the hall window. "The snow's tapering off, but drive carefully, Nancy."

"I will," Nancy said as she put on her coat. "And thanks for the hot chocolate."

She waved goodbye, and Suzanne shut the door behind her. The cold air stung Nancy's cheeks. Quickly, she walked through the snow to her car. She started the motor, then flicked on the lights. Nancy sat for a moment, thinking. Then she once again got out of the car. Putting the Moorelys' ladder away would give her an excuse to check out one more thing.

Nancy thought back to Paula's story. There were so many holes in it—the tracks in the snow, her unchanged clothes, the fastened chain lock, the open window, the doorbell no one answered.

In fact, all the evidence told Nancy that Paula was lying about being locked out. And Nancy knew that one final detail would confirm her suspicions.

She remembered that Paula had been carrying her big leather purse when she'd left the mall. If Paula had been sneaking in, she would have had to stash it somewhere before climbing onto the roof— somewhere safe and dry.

Nancy walked around the tree Paula had climbed and checked behind the bushes. Nothing. Nancy folded up the ladder and carried it into the garage. She propped it back in the corner, then glanced around.

28

The garage would be a perfect place to hide the purse. Nancy looked under a workbench, on top of shelves, and behind a mower. No bag. Maybe Paula's crazy story was true after all, Nancy thought. Then she spied a small trash can tucked in a shadowy corner.

Nancy crossed the garage and opened the lid. Bingo. There was Paula's leather bag.

4

Nasty Business

Nancy pulled the bag from the can. She recognized the fringed white leather. It was definitely the same bag Paula had been carrying in the mall.

That meant Paula had been sneaking into the house earlier. But why wouldn't she just admit it? And where had she been?

Maybe Suzanne had been right, Nancy thought. Paula could be in some kind of trouble.

Nancy stared at the purse. She was dying to look through it. The bag might hold a clue to where Paula had been that night.

But that was *really* snooping. Reluctantly, Nancy stuffed the purse back into the can. Then she frowned, wondering how the bag had been lying when she'd pulled it out.

Recalling that the side pocket had been facing up, Nancy turned the purse over. As she did, a green piece of paper fluttered to the ground. Nancy bent down and picked it up to examine it. One side was blank. When she flipped it over, she saw a serial number—7846-MT.

It seemed to be some kind of claim ticket. To a locker? A coat check in a restaurant? A parking garage?

Quickly, Nancy memorized the serial number. There was a chance it might be an important clue.

A clue to what? Nancy asked herself. So far she wasn't investigating anything. But she had to admit, Paula de Jagger's behavior was beginning to intrigue her.

Replacing the ticket, Nancy tucked the leather bag back into the trash can with the side pocket facing up. She set the lid on securely. Then she flicked off the garage light and shut the door.

The snow had stopped, and the sky was clearing. The moon peeped out from behind a cloud, casting its blue light across the yard.

As she opened the car door, Nancy glanced up at the roof, noticing how steep it was. Paula must have been desperate to try and make the climb.

Nancy's eyes followed the roofline to the second story. Something moved in Paula's window. Maybe it was a curtain being pulled back, Nancy thought as a chill raced up her spine. Had it been the shadow of a branch, or had Paula been watching her?

"Thanks for coming right over," Suzanne said, opening the Moorelys' front door the next afternoon. Grabbing Nancy's hands, she practically dragged her inside.

"Your phone call sounded pretty urgent," Nancy said as she slipped out of her coat. "What's going on?"

"It's about Paula," Suzanne replied. "She's at cheerleading practice right now, so Mom and I thought this would be a good time to talk."

"Hello. You must be Nancy Drew," Mrs. Moorely said as she walked down the hall toward the girls. She had gray-streaked red hair and wore a gray business suit. Worry lines creased her brow. "Suzanne and Bess have told me so much about you. I'm glad you could come so quickly. Why don't we sit down?"

Mrs. Moorely ushered Nancy into an immaculate living room. Nancy sat gingerly on the white sofa. She hoped she hadn't tracked snow onto the Oriental rug.

"I guess you know we're worried about Paula," Mrs. Moorely said after she sat down in a high-backed chair opposite Nancy. Suzanne perched on the arm of the chair.

"I told Mom about last night," Suzanne explained. "I didn't let on then, but I saw Paula on the roof. I didn't say anything because she's been so secretive lately."

"Paula didn't volunteer to explain what happened, so we didn't ask," Mrs. Moorely added. "We try to respect her privacy as much as possible."

"Paula told me she came downstairs to look at the snow and locked herself out," Nancy said.

"Hah!" Suzanne jumped up. "I don't believe that for a second. Last night I peeked in her room after you dropped me off. She'd padded her bed to make it look like she was sleeping."

"So she had been home?" Nancy asked.

Mrs. Moorely looked embarrassed. "We don't really know. My husband and I went to bed early. We thought Paula was with you girls."

"Obviously Miss Perfect had better plans," Suzanne grumbled.

"Now, Suzanne," Mrs. Moorely chided, "we don't know what Paula did. She may have had a good reason for not wanting us to know she'd been out late."

"You're always defending her," Suzanne said angrily. "You know as well as I do that something's up. Look at this."

Suzanne thrust an envelope toward Nancy. River Heights National Bank was printed on the top. "When I came home from school, I opened Paula's bank statement by mistake. And look." Suzanne pulled out the sheet of paper. "She's withdrawn almost all her money."

Nancy took the letter and envelope. Paula's name was clearly typed on it. Nancy wondered how Suzanne could have opened the statement by mistake. It looked as if she was trying to stir up trouble for Paula. Maybe it was Suzanne's way of getting her mother's attention. Or maybe she was trying to show her parents that Paula wasn't so perfect after all.

Whatever Suzanne's motive, Nancy decided she'd keep an eye on her.

Mrs. Moorely leaned forward. "Paula told us she wanted to save up her money to buy presents before she went home," she said.

"Could she have bought them already?" Nancy asked. Maybe there was a simple explanation for the missing money.

Suzanne shook her head. "She would have told us. Besides, she wanted my dad to help her pick out some of the electronic equipment."

Nancy tried again. "Well, maybe she's spending it on herself."

"Maybe." Mrs. Moorely frowned. "But her parents give her a very generous allowance."

"Over four hundred dollars a month!" Suzanne exclaimed. "Whew, what I could do with that much money."

"And we haven't noticed any new clothes, except what Paula brings home from the boutique," Mrs. Moorely went on. "Because she works so hard, the manager has been very generous." Mrs. Moorely sighed. "And my husband and I pay for the things we all do together. Paula really hasn't had to buy anything."

"You ought to see the jewelry she's gotten from Around the World," Suzanne said in a low voice. "Some really gorgeous necklaces."

Mrs. Moorely wrung her hands. "And this morning I overheard Paula on the phone to her parents. I know enough Dutch to have figured out she was asking for even more money. She wanted it as soon as possible."

Now Mrs. Moorely stood up and paced across the room. "When Paula hung up, her face was ashen. But when she saw me, she plastered on a fake smile." Suzanne's mother stopped in front of Nancy. "I just don't know what to think."

Nancy wasn't sure what to say. Paula was definitely acting strangely. But there still could be a logical explanation.

"Have you spoken with anyone in the exchange program?" Nancy asked. "Maybe they have an idea what's going on."

Mrs. Moorely nodded. "This morning, after the girls left for school, I called the regional coordinator, Larry Taylor. He was very nice. He told me Paula's behavior didn't sound that unusual. This time of year, many of the exchange students get homesick, but they don't want their year in the United States to end, either."

"So they're sad one minute and happy the next," Suzanne explained. "That does sound a little like Paula."

"What about the money?" Nancy asked.

"Mr. Taylor said that that wasn't unusual, either. So many things in America are cheaper than overseas that the exchange students go crazy. He thought Paula might be afraid to tell her parents she'd spent it all."

"Well, that makes sense," Nancy said. "I think

35

Mr. Taylor may have helped solve our little mystery."

"You're probably right." Mrs. Moorely sat down in her chair again and let out a relieved sigh. "Talking to you puts everything in perspective. I guess Suzanne and I jumped to the wrong conclusions."

"But what about Paula's weird behavior last night?" Suzanne pressed. "If *I'd* tried to sneak into the house, you and Dad would've grounded me for a month."

"That's because you're our daughter," Mrs. Moorely said with a smile. "You have to put up with your pesky parents. But don't worry, I'll talk to Paula about it. She probably has a good explanation."

"Oh, sure," Suzanne muttered. "Miss Perfect can do no wrong."

"Now, Suzanne," Mrs. Moorely scolded, "don't be silly." She stood up. "How about some homemade brownies?"

"Sounds great," the two girls chorused.

When her mother left, Suzanne looked at Nancy. "My mom thinks Paula's an angel, but I know better," she said, her eyes gleaming.

Nancy wondered what Suzanne meant. She knew Suzanne was disappointed that Paula had been cleared, at least for now. And the girl hadn't bothered to hide her jealousy. She'd certainly done everything possible to point out Paula's strange behavior.

Suzanne's behavior was raising a lot of questions in Nancy's mind. Had she locked Paula out on purpose? And why did Suzanne open the bank statement? Had she suspected something?

Nancy was about to ask her when the phone rang.

Suzanne sprang up. "I'll get it," she called into the kitchen. "Excuse me a minute," she said to Nancy as she dashed into the hall.

Nancy watched as Suzanne picked up the receiver. Suddenly the girl began waving wildly. She put her hand over the receiver. "Nancy, come here. Quick!"

Nancy jumped up and joined Suzanne in the hallway.

"It's him, the guy who keeps calling. You know — when Paula gets so weird. I'm going to pretend I'm Paula. You can get on the other phone and listen."

Nancy frowned. "Suzanne, I don't think that's such a good idea."

"It is if we want to find out if Paula is really in trouble," Suzanne insisted.

Nancy hesitated. Suzanne did have a point. If there was something going on, this might be their only chance to discover any clues about the caller.

"Okay," she agreed reluctantly. Suzanne pointed down the hall to the family phone, carefully covering the receiver with her palm.

"Hello, this is Paula," Suzanne said in Dutch.

Nancy was amazed at how much she sounded like the exchange student.

"Listen up," a hoarse voice said on the other end. "You blew it. Now you'll really pay."

Nancy heard Suzanne gasp.

"And if you don't," the voice went on, "the Moorelys will get a big surprise."

5

Danger Downtown

Nancy racked her brain to think of something to say—anything that would keep the caller on the line.

"What kind of surprise?" she whispered into the phone, trying to make her voice sound like Paula's.

But the line went dead.

Slowly, Nancy replaced the receiver.

"Nancy!" Suzanne came flying down the hallway into the family room. "What did that guy mean?" she asked anxiously. "Who do you think he was?"

"I have no idea," Nancy answered, shaking her head. "But one thing's for sure. Whoever it was meant business."

Suzanne shivered. "Wow. His voice gave me the creeps. He sounded like a foreign spy in a movie."

Nancy nodded. "You're right. He did have some kind of accent—British or Irish, maybe."

Suzanne gripped Nancy's wrist. "We have to find out what the surprise is. And what he meant when he said that Paula 'blew it.'"

Nancy nodded, then studied Suzanne. Could Suzanne have set up the call somehow? She'd been so eager to answer the phone.

"Do you have *any* idea who the caller was?" Nancy asked.

"No." Suzanne thought for a minute. "Paula has been hanging around with a rough-looking guy at school. You know, the leather-jacket type. He's got long blond hair. But I don't know if he's the caller."

Nancy remembered the guy she'd seen following Paula at the mall. He'd worn a ski jacket, though, and had short dark hair. "What's his name?"

"Shaun Devane," Suzanne replied immediately. "Maybe she was out with him last night."

"Don't you think she would have told you?" Nancy asked. She and Bess and George told each other everything they did.

"A month ago Paula might have, but lately she's been really secretive. And Shaun's not the kind of guy my parents would be wild about."

Mrs. Moorely bustled into the family room, carrying a plate of brownies. "Thank goodness for the microwave," she said as she passed them around. "Homebaked brownies in a jiffy."

Nancy took a bite. "Mmm. They're delicious."

"Who was the phone call for?" Mrs. Moorely asked, setting the brownies on the table.

"Umm . . ." Suzanne hesitated.

40

Mrs. Moorely glanced from one girl to the other. "Is something wrong?"

"We're not sure," Nancy said slowly. Then she told Suzanne's mother about the phone call.

Mrs. Moorely frowned and sat down on the sofa. Suzanne quickly went to sit next to her. "It could just be a crank call," Mrs. Moorely said after a moment.

"But just in case Paula might be in trouble, I'd like you and Suzanne to tell me everything you know about her," Nancy said.

"I can't believe Paula might be in trouble," Mrs. Moorely said. "She's been a wonderful addition to the household." Then she launched into a glowing description of the exchange student.

Nancy watched Suzanne's mouth droop lower and lower as her mother talked. "How about places and kids she hangs out with?" Nancy asked.

"Sometimes Paula goes to Le Café after work," Suzanne piped up. "With the cheerleaders," she added. "Of course, I'm never invited."

Suzanne's mother didn't seem to notice the bitterness in her daughter's voice.

"And you know about the boutique," Mrs. Moorely added. "Three or four afternoons a week Paula catches the downtown bus from school. She gets to work about four o'clock."

"That might be a good time to catch up to her," Nancy said. "I'm going to find out all I can and get back to you. I'm afraid I'd better be going." Nancy stood up. "Thanks for the brownies. And call me if you get any more phone calls."

Mrs. Moorely smiled and took Nancy's hand. "Thank you for all of your help. I feel better already. How about you, Suzanne?"

"I feel great!" Suzanne exclaimed. "I mean," she said quickly, "I feel great that Nancy's helping us. Now we just need to find out about that phone call."

Nancy put on her coat and headed toward the hall. But before she reached the front door, Suzanne caught her sleeve. "I'll call you if anything else comes up," the redhead whispered, her eyes glowing.

Nancy thought Suzanne seemed awfully eager. Was it possible she was glad that Paula might be in trouble?

"I wonder what's keeping Paula," Nancy said, drumming her fingers on the back of the car seat. She checked her watch. "School was out fifteen minutes ago."

"Boy, do I remember counting the seconds till that bell rang," Bess said from the passenger seat. "Last period I had algebra with Mr. MacDonald, remember?"

Nancy laughed. "Your favorite teacher."

The girls had parked across the street from River Heights High School, hoping to catch Paula before she left. The night before, Nancy had decided that the best way to get to the bottom of the mystery was to talk directly to Paula.

"When we do see her, act casual," Nancy told Bess. "That way, maybe she'll buy our story about being here to pick up some old school records. Then we'll offer her a ride to work."

"Are you going to come right out and ask Paula about that phone call?" Bess asked.

Nancy sighed. "I'm not sure. She certainly doesn't seem eager to talk about anything. This is all we have so far." Nancy counted off the clues on her fingers: "Paula trying to climb in her window, the guy who might have been following Paula at the mall, a depleted bank account, and a threatening phone call. That's not much to go on."

Bess said nothing.

"And Suzanne complicates things," Nancy continued. "She's so jealous, it's hard to decide what's real and what she's making up."

"I know Suzanne pretty well," Bess said, "and I don't think she'd lie. Exaggerate, yes." Bess chuckled. "And she does have a temper."

"That's one more reason to talk to Paula." Craning her neck, Nancy looked for the exchange student again. Finally, she spotted Paula stepping out of the school building.

"There she is." Nancy rolled down the car window to wave. Then she saw that Paula wasn't alone. Beside her was a good-looking guy wearing a black leather jacket. His longish blond hair was pulled back in a ponytail.

"That must be Shaun Devane," Nancy whispered excitedly. "He fits Suzanne's description perfectly."

"I remember him!" Bess exclaimed. "He was in

43

one of my classes. He seemed smart, but he hung around with a pretty tough crowd."

Nancy watched Suzanne and Shaun walk slowly toward the parking lot. They appeared to be deep in conversation. As they moved closer, Nancy rolled the window back up and hunched into her seat.

"Scoot down," she whispered to Bess. "I want to watch them together."

It looked as if the two of them were arguing. Paula was frowning and shaking her head. Shaun was gesturing wildly. Nancy wished she could hear what they were saying. She squinted, trying to read their lips.

Why not? Shaun seemed to be asking. His brow was furrowed.

Again, Paula shook her head emphatically. Then, clasping her books tightly to her chest, she turned and hurried away.

Shaun slapped his leg, obviously frustrated. Muttering something under his breath, he strode toward a motorcycle in the parking lot.

Paula crossed the street several cars in front of Nancy's car and stopped beside a bus sign. After a few minutes the downtown bus pulled up with a squeal of brakes. At the same time, the motorcycle roared to life. Without glancing right or left, Paula climbed onto the bus. The motorcycle zoomed from the parking lot, then slowed behind the bus.

Nancy started her car. "It looks like Shaun's going to follow the bus," she said. "Maybe we can find out where they're going."

Bess strapped on her seat belt. "Oh, good. The chase is on!"

The bus headed into downtown River Heights. After following it three blocks, the motorcycle turned right. The bus stopped at a light, then continued straight.

"Hmmm. I wonder why Shaun took off in a different direction," Nancy mused aloud.

"And Paula's not going to work," Bess added. "The mall is to the left."

"Let's find out where she's headed," Nancy said.

Just then, the bus stopped at a corner and the blond girl jumped off. Still clutching her books, Paula hurried down the sidewalk. Nancy scanned the storefronts. Her gaze settled on a sign that read River Heights National Bank.

So that was Paula's destination, Nancy thought as she pulled into an empty parking place just as Paula went into the bank.

Nancy remembered what Mrs. Moorely had said about Paula's phone call to her parents. She'd asked for more money and wanted it fast. Nancy knew it was possible for the de Jaggers to have wired the money directly to the bank. Maybe Paula was withdrawing it already.

"The bank?" Bess questioned, raising her eyebrows.

Nancy nodded. "Paula seems desperate for money. My guess is, someone's blackmailing her."

Bess sucked in her breath. "Do you think it's Shaun Devane?"

45

"Maybe," Nancy said, shrugging. "His name is Irish. He could have been the mysterious caller."

A few minutes later, Paula emerged from the bank. Stopping on the steps, she peered into a small white envelope. Then she crossed the street right in front of a car.

Nancy gasped as the car slammed on its brakes and honked. Paula looked up distractedly.

"That was a close call!" Bess exclaimed. The exchange student hurried down the sidewalk and into the River Heights Post Office.

Nancy remembered the caller's strange words: "Now you'll really pay." Was Paula about to pay him off?

"Stay here," Nancy said to Bess, jumping from the car.

She crossed the street and entered the post office. It was filled with people, so Nancy was able to blend easily into the crowd. Pulling her coat collar around her neck, she wound her way past a group of people until she was standing almost behind Paula. A woman wearing a bulky parka and carrying a poodle stood between them. Paula would never see her.

When Paula reached the clerk, Nancy peered around the poodle, trying to see her. Baring his sharp teeth, the little dog growled menacingly at Nancy. Surprised, she stepped backward.

The dog's owner gave Nancy a nasty look. "Now, Fifi, you be a darling," she crooned to the poodle.

Nancy rolled her eyes, then peeked over the lady's other shoulder. She could see the bank envelope in Paula's hand. A money order was sticking out from the top.

"I'd like to send this overnight express," she heard Paula say.

The clerk handed Paula a big cardboard envelope. As Paula filled in the address label, Nancy stood on her tiptoes, trying to see. But the blond girl was huddled over the envelope. There was no way Nancy could make out what she wrote.

Nancy watched as Paula slipped the money order inside the cardboard envelope and handed it to the clerk. He ripped off the receipt and gave it to her.

"Thank you," Paula said, and turned to go. Nancy ducked behind the woman just as Paula passed her and stepped quickly through the door.

Nancy racked her brain. She had to get a look at the envelope.

The woman with the dog stepped up to the counter where Paula had just stood, and this gave Nancy an idea.

"What a cute little dog," Nancy said quickly, stepping next to the woman. She reached up to pat Fifi's fluffy head. Just as she'd hoped, the little dog snapped at her.

With feigned horror, Nancy screamed and fell sideways against the counter.

"Get away from my Fifi!" the lady screeched, tightening her grip on the poodle. "You're scaring the poor thing."

Snarling angrily, the dog struggled out of the woman's arms and jumped to the floor. The flustered clerk dropped Paula's envelope on the counter. Quickly, Nancy read what was written on the envelope—"care of Mr. and Mrs. Stephen Chester."

The woman lifted up the yapping dog. Before the clerk whisked Paula's envelope into the bin, Nancy had memorized the zip code.

Now she had to go after Paula. Nancy didn't want to lose her.

But when she got outside, the blond girl was nowhere in sight. Nancy checked in both directions and across the street. Where had the exchange student gone?

Just then, Nancy heard a muffled scream. It was coming from the alley next to the post office.

Nancy raced to the entrance and turned the corner. Then she stopped dead in her tracks.

Paula de Jagger was lying in the middle of the alley, her eyes wide with fright. And bending over her was Shaun Devane!

6

Information, Please

"Stop right there!" Nancy screamed. Rushing forward, she grabbed Shaun's arm and spun him backward. He fell against the alley wall.

"Leave her alone or I'll call the police," she said breathlessly.

"Wait!" Paula struggled onto her elbows. "Shaun was just trying to help me."

Nancy stared at the blond girl, then at Shaun. He was looking back at her in shocked silence. Finally, he raised his hands in mock surrender.

"Paula's right," he said. "I found her sprawled in the alley. I was reaching down to help her up, okay?"

"That's not what it looked like to me." Nancy glared at him as she kneeled next to Paula. The exchange student's face was white and her lips were pursed in a thin line. Her gaze darted nervously down the narrow alley.

Nancy looked over Paula's shoulder. The other end opened into a parking lot. She thought she heard the faint sound of retreating footsteps.

"Are you all right?" Nancy asked, turning her attention back to Paula.

Shaking her head, the blond girl pointed to her right leg. "I twisted my ankle. Stupid me. I was in a hurry and slipped on the ice."

"Let me check it." Nancy unzipped Paula's boot and put gentle pressure on the ankle. "It feels okay. Why don't you see if you can walk on it?" She held out her hand to Paula.

"Here, let me help." Shaun bent down and put his arm around Paula's shoulders. Nancy steadied her, and the two of them lifted Paula to her feet.

The exchange student gave Nancy a grateful smile. "This is the second time you've had to rescue me. Thanks."

Nancy shrugged. "No problem. I was headed for the post office when I saw you . . . and Shaun." Nancy gave him a pointed look.

"It wasn't Shaun's fault," Paula repeated. "Snow and I just don't seem to get along."

What snow? Nancy thought grimly. A clean path had been shoveled down the alley so that patrons could walk to their cars. Sand and salt had been sprinkled on the few remaining icy spots.

Nancy tested the footing with her boot. It would have been hard to slip. And Paula didn't look that clumsy.

Nancy glanced suspiciously at Shaun Devane. He

was watching Paula closely, a frown on his face. An earring glinted in one ear, and his handsome face was marred by a sullen, almost angry expression.

Had he knocked Paula down? Paula had looked so frightened and nervous. Was she scared of Shaun Devane? Or had someone else met Paula outside the post office, roughed her up, and then escaped?

Shaun's motorcycle was parked in front of the alley. He might have seen someone disappearing the other way, Nancy thought, looking over at him.

"Hey, I'm innocent." He glared at Nancy. "And I didn't see any goons running off, either. If Paula said she slipped, then she slipped. Right, Paula?"

The blond girl's face flushed pink. She nodded emphatically. "Oh, yes, I'm so uncoordinated. I'm all left feet."

I doubt that, Nancy thought. Suzanne had told her Paula was a fantastic cheerleader, and cheerleaders were usually good athletes.

But why would Paula lie? And why did Shaun seem so angry?

"Who are *you*, anyway?" Shaun asked suddenly in an accusing voice. He took a step forward, his hands clenched into fists.

Paula touched his arm. "She's a friend of Suzanne's," she reassured him. "Nancy Drew, this is Shaun Devane. Now why don't you guys shake hands and make up?"

Reluctantly, Nancy offered her hand. She wasn't too sure about Shaun Devane. He acted as if he had a big chip on his shoulder.

51

"Come on, Paula, I'll take you to work," Shaun said abruptly. Putting his hand under her elbow, he steered her toward the motorcycle. Hesitantly, Paula walked on her ankle.

"Just a second." Nancy's voice was firm. "I think Paula should ride in a car after all that's happened. That way, she can stay off her foot."

"She's right, Shaun," Paula said. "Besides, I'd freeze to death on your motorcycle. I don't know how you ride on that thing all winter."

Shaun frowned, then dropped his arm. "Okay. But I still need to talk to you, Paula. *Soon.*" His blue eyes drilled into hers. Then he turned and strode off toward his motorcycle.

"What was that all about?" Nancy asked.

"Nothing," Paula said quickly. "I've been helping him with some of his classes. He didn't do too well in school last year. Now he's trying to get on the honor roll."

"Really?" Nancy said. She found it hard to believe that Shaun and Paula had been discussing a tutoring session. "Well, that's great. I hope he makes it."

"Me, too." Paula smiled. "Listen, Nancy, we'd better get going, or I'll be late for work."

Nancy took Paula's elbow, supporting her weight as they walked toward the street. After a few steps, Paula began walking normally, but her face was still pale.

Nancy checked both ways, then guided Paula over to her car.

"Hey! What's going on?" Bess waved from the

entrance of a nearby coffee shop. She had a bag in her hand.

"Paula fell," Nancy told her shortly as she opened the car door. Paula slid into the front seat.

"And where have you been?" Nancy asked Bess in a whisper after she'd shut the door.

Bess shrugged. "I got hungry waiting for you and went to get something to eat. Why?"

"I'll tell you later," Nancy said.

The two got into the car, Bess climbing into the back seat. Paula was quiet as Nancy started the engine.

"Anyone want a doughnut?" Bess asked.

"No, thanks," Nancy answered.

Paula didn't say anything. Glancing over, Nancy saw that the exchange student was staring out the window, a glazed expression on her face. Her hands were clasped in her lap, and she was chewing nervously on her lip.

Nancy could tell that something was going on. The "fall" had obviously shaken Paula, but Nancy had a feeling there was more to it than that. She wondered if Paula would confide in her. So far, she'd evaded all of Nancy's questions. Still, she had to try.

Nancy touched Paula on the shoulder. "Are you all right?" she asked gently. "You seem worried."

Paula jumped as if she'd been given an electric shock. "Me?" she asked with false gaiety. "I'm just great. My ankle hurts a little, that's all."

"Are you sure?" Nancy raised her brows. "I mean, I'd like to help if there's something wrong."

"I . . ." For a moment, Paula hesitated. A shadow darkened her blue eyes, and she opened her mouth as if she were about to say something.

Good, Nancy thought, she's going to let me in on what's bothering her. Then maybe we can solve this mystery once and for all.

But then Paula smiled brightly. "Oh, it's nothing," she said. "I was just wondering what I'm going to do about cheerleading practice tomorrow. My ankle may be too sore."

"Oh." Nancy felt like a balloon that had just been deflated. With a sigh of frustration, she pulled the car into traffic.

After she'd dropped Paula off at the mall, Nancy told Bess about Paula's questionable accident.

"Do you think it was Shaun?" Bess asked.

Nancy shook her head. "Something tells me he wasn't lying—at least about that. And he can't be our mysterious caller, unless he knows how to fake an Irish accent."

"So what do you think happened?"

"I think someone else knew Paula was going to be at the post office. He or she met her outside and pulled her into the alley." Nancy frowned at Bess. "Did you see anyone suspicious hanging around?"

Bess looked sheepish. "To tell you the truth, I was having such a hard time deciding between jelly-filled or chocolate doughnuts that I didn't pay much attention to anything else."

Nancy had to laugh. "Some detective you are. Luckily for you, I did find out one thing this afternoon. Paula sent a money order to someone. I got a name and the zip code off the envelope."

"Wow!" Bess exclaimed. Then she looked puzzled. "So, now what do we do?"

Nancy grinned as she turned her car into the Drews' driveway. "You'll see." The girls entered the house. After a brief stop in the kitchen to grab two diet sodas, Nancy led the way to her father's study.

Nancy pulled several phone books from the desk. "We'll soon find out if Mr. and Mrs. Stephen Chester live near here," she told Bess as she handed her a phone book opened to the zip code page. She recited the zip code from the envelope, and the two girls started searching.

Finally Bess said, "I've got it!"

Nancy looked to where Bess was pointing, and saw that the zip code was for the town of Joliet, which meant that Mr. and Mrs. Chester lived only about an hour's drive from River Heights.

Immediately, Nancy picked up the phone and dialed long-distance information.

"I'd like the number for Mr. Stephen Chester in Joliet," she said, crossing her fingers. The computerized voice clicked on. "The number is 555-3099. Please make a note of it."

Nancy scrawled the number on a piece of scrap paper. "Well, that was easy. The hard part will be convincing Mr. and Mrs. Chester to answer a few questions."

Bess grinned. "Why don't you try the direct

approach. Like, are you blackmailing Paula de Jagger?"

Nancy laughed at her friend as she dialed. A woman's cheerful voice answered the phone on the first ring. Nancy could hear the TV blaring in the background and the rush of running water.

"Hello! Is this Mrs. Chester?" Nancy asked in a hearty voice.

"Yes," the woman replied.

"Mrs. Chester, you have been randomly selected to participate in a survey for Telemarketing, Inc. We'd like to ask you some questions about your favorite salad dressings."

"Salad dressings? Why, sure." The water stopped. "My husband and I are both on diets, so we eat salad every night."

"That's great," Nancy said, thinking fast. "Should I limit my questions to lo-cal dressings?"

"Oh, heavens, no." Mrs. Chester laughed. "They're so bland. We like the blue cheese and sour cream type."

"That's wonderful," Nancy said brightly. "The company I'm representing is marketing new ranch and creamy Italian dressings. Would you like to receive free samples?"

"My, yes!" Mrs. Chester replied eagerly.

"Let me get your address."

Mrs. Chester rattled it off, and Nancy took down the information.

"Now, before I go, I'd like to get some information for our files," Nancy went on. "How many members are there in your household?"

"Three," the woman replied. "My husband, myself, and my son. Oh, yes, and we also have an exchange student living with us."

Nancy's ears pricked up. "That must be exciting," she gushed. "When I was in high school, my family had an exchange student from London. Where is yours from?"

"Neil's from a small town in the west of Ireland. And what a dear he's been."

Nancy's mind raced. Neil was from Ireland. She'd suspected that the mysterious caller who'd threatened the Moorelys had an Irish accent.

"Well, I hope Neil enjoys the dressings. You should be receiving them in three weeks."

"Thank you so much," Mrs. Chester said. "We'll look forward to it."

"And thank you, Mrs. Chester," Nancy said gleefully as she hung up. "Bingo!" she said as she picked up the phone again and dialed the Moorelys' number. "Now I need to find out from Suzanne or her mom if Paula knew or has ever talked about an exchange student named Neil."

Bess shook her head. "You're amazing, Nancy."

The Moorelys' line was busy. Nancy pressed the button, then impatiently dialed again. Still busy.

"So Paula's sending money to an exchange student named Neil?" Bess asked when Nancy hung up.

"It looks that way," Nancy said. "Either he's the mysterious caller or a friend in trouble." She checked her watch. It was after six-thirty, and her stomach was beginning to growl. Picking up the phone, she tried one last time. "If it's still busy, I'm driving over."

The busy signal buzzed in her ear. Nancy slammed the receiver down and grabbed her coat from the chair.

"Can you drop me off on the way?" Bess asked. "My parents are having company and want me to meet them."

"You mean, your mom's fixing a terrific dinner and you want to be there," Nancy joked.

Bess laughed. "Something like that."

On their way out, the girls passed through the kitchen. Hannah Gruen, the Drews' housekeeper, had left a note and a sandwich. Hannah had been with the Drews ever since Nancy's mom had died when Nancy was young.

The note said, "Your father's at a meeting. I'm at the Oswalds' playing bridge. Don't forget to eat!" Nancy picked up the sandwich and took a bite. Mmm. Turkey on rye. She plucked a can of juice from the refrigerator.

Bess licked her lips and gazed hungrily at the sandwich.

Nancy gave her the other half, and the girls headed for the car.

Nancy's sandwich was long gone by the time she dropped off Bess and turned down the Moorelys' street. Nancy was taking one last sip of juice when a fire engine's siren blasted right behind her. With a jerk, she zipped her car over to the curb just as a River Heights fire truck zoomed past. Then she saw the fire engines, cars, and people clustered at the end of the street.

Nancy choked down her drink. Driving closer, she parked behind an ambulance. Jumping from the car, she pushed her way past several onlookers and continued up the sidewalk toward a yellow house. Smoke and flames billowed from the basement window.

The Moorelys' house was on fire!

7

After the Fire

"Is anyone hurt?" Nancy asked a fireman who was keeping people away from the burning house. Anxiously, she scanned the crowd, looking for the Moorelys.

"Nope. Everyone got out in time," the fireman replied. "The fire was pretty much confined to the basement. It's about out by now."

Nancy spied Suzanne huddled against her mother by the fire chief's car. A blanket was wrapped around the two of them. A man wearing slippers and a sweater was talking to the fire chief. Nancy figured he was Mr. Moorely.

She didn't see Paula and hoped she was still at work.

Nancy's mind raced back to the mysterious caller's threatening words: "You blew it. Now you'll really pay. And if you don't, the Moorelys will get a big surprise."

Could the fire be the surprise? Nancy shivered as she watched the firemen hose down the outside walls of the house. If it was, then Paula was in way over her head. The caller wasn't a kid playing a prank. He meant business.

This time, no one had been hurt. But what about the next time?

Suddenly Suzanne spied Nancy. Tossing the blanket off her shoulders, the redhead rushed across the yard. Her face was white beneath the freckles. Nancy stepped from the crowd to meet her.

"Nancy, this is terrible!" Suzanne cried, her voice shaking. "This is what the guy on the phone meant!" A tear trickled down her cheek. Sniffing, she wiped it away.

"It could be, but we don't know that for sure." Nancy threw an arm around Suzanne and hugged her. "Is your family all right?"

Suzanne nodded. "Paula's at work, so she wasn't even here!" There was a touch of anger in her voice.

"Let's not blame this on Paula," Nancy said.

"You're right," Suzanne said in a hushed voice. Nancy could feel her trembling. "Paula really is in trouble, and we need to help her."

"Yes." Nancy pulled a tissue from her pocket, and Suzanne blew her nose.

"It's all my fault. I wanted Paula to be in trouble." She began crying harder. "I wanted my parents to see she wasn't so perfect after all. I knew Paula needed money. She tried to borrow some from me. That's why I opened her bank statement."

61

"Hey." Nancy squeezed her shoulder. "I understand. And there's no way this fire is your fault. If someone did set it, you couldn't have stopped it."

"I guess." Suzanne sniffled loudly. "But I didn't help Paula enough. I knew she was out that night, so I locked the door. I thought she'd have to ring the bell and wake up my parents. Then maybe they'd ground her or something."

"I'm afraid being grounded is the least of Paula's worries." Nancy looked up at the Moorelys' house. It looked as if the fire was completely out, but the smell of wet, charred wood and smoke filled the air.

"You'll help her, won't you?" Suzanne asked.

Nancy nodded. "And you can, too." Nancy was glad to see that Suzanne had undergone a change of heart where Paula was concerned. The fire had obviously convinced Suzanne that Paula was in serious trouble and needed help. "You know Paula better than anyone," Nancy said. "Come on, let's go talk to your mom."

The girls started across the snow-covered lawn. Mrs. Moorely greeted them with outstretched arms.

"I'm so sorry," Nancy said.

"We're just happy no one's hurt." Mrs. Moorely took the blanket from her shoulders and draped it over Suzanne. "Fortunately, the fire was confined to the basement, but there's smoke damage everywhere."

"Do you know what's happened?" Nancy asked.

Mrs. Moorely shook her head. "My husband's been talking to the fire chief, but so far they haven't determined the cause."

A few moments later, Mr. Moorely came up, and Suzanne introduced him to Nancy. He said hello, then stared in disbelief at the firemen carrying furniture from the house.

"I just don't get it," he said, shaking his head. "Chief Nelson said the source of the fire was a bunch of gas-soaked rags near the furnace. I told him that was crazy."

"We'd never be that careless," Mrs. Moorely agreed.

"It may not have been your fault," Nancy reassured them. "Paula's mysterious caller mentioned a surprise. This may be it."

"Maybe," Mr. Moorely said. "It could be an accident, though. Maybe the workmen left rags when we had our house painted, and I missed them."

"And we were home all evening," Mrs. Moorely added. "We never heard a thing, and we keep the basement locked. Besides, who on earth would want to hurt us?"

"We'd better tell the police," Mr. Moorely said wearily.

"I'll let Chief Nelson know about the call," Nancy offered. "He'll notify the police if it's arson. But I think we should keep Paula's name out of this if possible."

"That way, Nancy can find out what kind of trouble she's in," Suzanne said. "Nancy's an experienced detective," she told her dad. "She's solved all sorts of tricky cases."

"All right, Ms. Drew." Mr. Moorely ran his

fingers through his thinning hair. "I hope you can get to the bottom of this thing. My family doesn't need any more surprises."

"I agree," Nancy told him. Just then, she caught sight of Paula stepping through the crowd. When the blond girl saw what had happened, she froze in her tracks and clapped her hands to her mouth.

Paula's eyes welled with tears as she stared with horror at the house and all the firemen. When she saw the Moorelys, she quickly wiped her cheeks and raced over to them.

"What happened?" she cried. "Are you all right?"

"Yes, we're all right, and we're glad you are, too," Suzanne said with relief.

Suddenly, a medic from the rescue squad rushed up to them. "Are you folks ready to go to the hospital?"

"Hospital?" Mr. Moorely echoed. "We're all fine."

The medic shook his head. "You think you're fine, but smoke inhalation can be tricky. You'll need to get checked out."

"I'm going with you," Paula said.

"We want you with us." Mrs. Moorely linked her arm in Paula's. Suzanne took Paula's other arm.

For a few moments, everyone watched as the firemen brought out what was left of the things from the basement. Soon a smoldering pile of chairs, rugs, boxes, and books was stacked on the lawn.

"My old doll carriage!" Suzanne cried. She ran

over to the stack. The rest of the family joined her to stare in dismay at their ruined things.

"Well, I always wanted to redo the basement," Mrs. Moorely said, trying to sound cheerful. "Now's my chance."

"And to think I just painted the house bright yellow." Mr. Moorely sighed. "I guess I should have left it gray. It would have matched the smoke."

His wife and daughter laughed weakly at his joke, but Nancy could tell their hearts weren't in it. Soon, the Moorelys turned to follow the medic toward the emergency service vehicle.

Paula lingered for a minute, staring at several books lying in a charred heap. They were still smoldering.

Suddenly, she reached into her pocket and pulled out a folded sheet of paper. She crumpled it into a ball, then tossed it on top of the books. She watched as the paper began to smoke. When it started to flame, she spun around and hurried after the Moorelys.

Almost without thinking, Nancy rushed forward and kicked the paper into the snow. Then she stomped on it with her boot.

"Hey!" a fireman hollered. "Get back. This stuff could still flare up."

"Sorry," Nancy called back. Quickly, she bent down and picked up the paper. The edges crumpled into black ashes and floated away in the wind. She folded the rest of the paper carefully and slipped it into her purse.

Nancy backed into the thinning crowd and found a dark spot behind a fire truck. She pulled the paper and her pocket flashlight from her purse. Flicking the light on, she studied the paper.

It was a letter printed out by a word processor. Unfortunately, the top address and bottom signature were missing, and the body of the letter was so burned that Nancy couldn't make out whole sentences.

"Inez, whose home is Essen, Germany, wishes to visit . . . Also, please remember to go to . . . drive up to New York was . . . wishes to thank Pablo . . . will not be able to smoke . . ."

Nancy frowned. It appeared that the paper was nothing more than a newsletter or bulletin for the students in Paula's exchange program. Why would Paula want to burn it?

Nancy shoved the note back into her purse. There had to be a reason. She'd check the paper more carefully when she had better light.

Frustrated, Nancy strode from the shadows back to the lawn. She was tired of half-clues and what-ifs. She wanted to find out for sure if the fire had been an accident. And she didn't want to wait for the results of the fire chief's investigation.

The firemen had finished carrying the furniture out the front door. Some of the men were huddled together talking. Others were rolling up hoses and stashing equipment back in the fire trucks. Chief Nelson was calling out orders.

Making sure no one was watching her, Nancy doubled back behind the vehicles and crossed the neighbor's yard. Then she ducked around the Moorelys' garage and ran to the back of their house.

Nancy knew that checking the snow for footprints would be a waste of time. There were too many of them already. She studied the back of the house. The entrance to the basement was down a set of concrete steps in a stairwell. The firemen had left the door open. Nancy went down the stairs and inspected the door and lock. There were no signs of tampering.

She climbed back up and then stepped backward to scan the outside walls. There were two small windows, one on each side of the stairway. Both were shut tight. Except for the blackened glass, the windows looked normal.

So how had the arsonist gotten in? If there was an arsonist, Nancy reminded herself.

She walked slowly down a snow-covered walkway that led around the corner of the basement. Bushes lined the side wall. Nancy bent down and parted the branches. Hidden behind them was a third window set in a deep well.

Kneeling in the snow, Nancy inched her way under the prickly bushes. When she was able to sit up, she faced the window and felt along the glass with her gloved hand. There it was. A perfectly round hole about four inches in diameter had been made with a glass cutter.

Carefully, Nancy felt inside the hole with two fingers. Twisting her hand, she was able to grab the inside latch and turn it.

The latch released. Nancy pushed the window

open. With a little maneuvering, even a full-grown man would have been able to squeeze through the window.

Nancy had her answer. Someone had broken into the Moorelys' basement and set the fire. Now she had to find out who the person was.

She studied the ground under the window. The intruder had carefully brushed the snow away so he or she wouldn't leave any footprints. That meant the arsonist was probably too smart to leave fingerprints, but Nancy wanted to check to make sure.

Then a sudden noise made her freeze. *Crunch. Crunch.* Someone was walking through the snow, moving slowly so no one would hear him.

Nancy held her breath, her heart pounding so hard she could feel it in her throat. *Crunch. Crunch.* The footsteps slowed, then stopped. Nancy parted the branches. In the dark, she could just make out two pants legs silhouetted against the snow.

Then there was a click, and a beam of light flashed into the bushes, blinding her. Nancy shrank back against the basement wall. There was no way she could escape.

8

A Revealing Message

Nancy threw up her arm to shield her eyes from the blinding light.

"Got you!" a man's voice snarled as a gloved hand reached in and grabbed Nancy's wrist. With one yank, the hand pulled her through the bushes.

"Let go!" Nancy gave the arm a swift chop, then kicked the man in the knee.

"Ow! Hey!" He dropped her arm and clutched his knee. Nancy scrambled backward, slipped on the snow, and fell down with a thump.

Quickly, she jumped to her feet, just as the man straightened up. Angry eyes glared at her from under a ski cap.

Nancy recognized his ruddy cheeks immediately. It was Officer Brody, a rookie member of the River Heights police force. Brody had guarded a valuable brooch from a vengeful crook during one of Nancy's recent cases. He'd also let the thief get away.

"What in the . . . ? Nancy Drew, what are you doing skulking around in the bushes?" he growled. "I almost slapped cuffs on you."

"What am *I* doing? What about you, sneaking around the Moorelys' house without your police uniform on?" Nancy bent down and angrily brushed the snow off her coat and pants. She couldn't believe she had let this inexperienced officer frighten her.

He chuckled. "Oh, excuse me—I forgot. It's Detective Drew, isn't it? I bet you're on another case," he added.

"That's right," Nancy grumbled.

"Well, I'm not telling you anything until you tell me what you're doing here." Officer Brody folded his arms.

"All right," Nancy agreed. She bent down and parted the bushes. "There's a window back here. Shine your flashlight on the glass."

Officer Brody whistled when he saw the hole. "Pretty clean-looking job. Looks as if Chief Nelson was right."

Nancy raised her eyebrows. "So he did suspect arson. I guess that's why he called the police."

Officer Brody shrugged. "All the facts aren't in yet."

"What facts?" Nancy flicked on her own flashlight and shone it in the young man's face. "You promised to tell me what you know," she reminded him.

Officer Brody flinched. "Okay, okay. The burned

rags they found had been twisted to make a torch."
He nodded toward the hole. "And that window
takes the heat off the Moorelys. You always have to
suspect the owners first. Plenty of so-called up-
standing citizens burn down their houses or stores
to collect the insurance money." He stopped,
frowning. "Of course, the Moorelys could've tried
to make it look like someone broke in."

"I don't think so," Nancy said. "But you'll let me
know what their insurance company says, right?"

"Uh . . ." He hesitated. "It depends on what's in
it for me. Do you know anything else about the
fire?"

Nancy told him about the mysterious call, but she
left out Paula's name.

"Sounds like some kook," the officer said. "I
hope River Heights isn't going to have a rash of fires
breaking out now."

"Me, too." Nancy slipped her flashlight back into
her purse and shivered as the wind howled around
the corner of the house. The back of her pants was
soaked from her fall in the snow.

Officer Brody pulled his cap over his ears. "Well,
Detective Drew, I have a job to do."

"Mind if I tag along?" Nancy asked.

"Yes, I do." Taking Nancy's arm, Officer Brody
marched her to the front yard. "Now run along like
a good girl and leave the rest of this investigation to
a real police officer. Good night, Detective Drew."

Nancy gritted her teeth. "Good night, Officer
Brody," she said in a mocking tone.

As she headed for her car, Nancy saw that the fire trucks were pulling away. Most of the bystanders had already left.

She checked her watch when she reached her car. It was ten o'clock. She was just unlocking the door when she noticed a red sports coupe parked along the curb on the other side of the street. Someone was leaning out the driver's window, looking at the Moorelys' house.

Nancy recognized the person immediately. It was the dark-haired guy she'd seen at the mall—the one she'd thought was following Paula. Casually, Nancy let go of the key, turned around, and started across the street. The young man was staring so intently at the house that he didn't notice Nancy until she was almost next to the car.

"Hi! You're a friend of Paula's, aren't you?" Nancy asked.

When the young man looked up, startled, his face paled. Fear flared in his green eyes. Quickly, he ducked his head back into his car and started the motor.

"Hey! Wait a minute." Nancy reached for the door handle. "I'm a friend of Paula's, too."

The red car roared to life. Nancy peered in at the driver. Quickly, she noted that he was about her age. He was wearing the same ski jacket he'd had on at the mall.

Then, without a word, the young man floored the gas pedal. The car leaped forward, and he shot her a nervous look over his shoulder.

"Wait," she pleaded. "I only want to ask you a couple of questions."

The tires spun wildly, sending clumps of slushy ice flying through the air. Wet snow flew in her face. She wiped it away, but not before the red car had careened around the corner.

Rats! She didn't even get a license plate number. With a groan, Nancy looked down at her coat, pants, and boots. She was splattered from head to toe with grimy, day-old snow. She was soaking wet both front and back.

She returned to her car and turned the heater on full blast. Freezing cold air whooshed over her numb feet. It wasn't until she pulled into her own driveway that warm air came out of the vents.

Nancy was still shivering when she slipped off her coat. Carson Drew met her in the hall.

"What happened to you?" With a worried frown, he took his daughter's coat and hung it up. Then he held her icy hands in his.

"Well, lucky for you, Hannah made chicken soup," Mr. Drew said as he led Nancy into the kitchen. He steered her toward a chair. "I'll get some for you."

Nancy nodded. "Thanks," she said, her teeth chattering.

Her father put the steaming bowl of soup on the table, and Nancy sat down.

"So what was so important that you spent all night running around in twenty-degree weather?" he asked after she'd swallowed several spoonfuls.

73

"The Moorelys' house caught fire," Nancy said between sips. "Remember that threatening phone call they got? Well, according to Chief Nelson, the fire today was no accident."

Mr. Drew listened quietly as Nancy told the whole story.

"Do you suspect blackmail?" he asked.

Nancy nodded. "Paula made a payment to someone." She paused, frowning. "So why would the blackmailer set the house on fire?" she wondered aloud.

"It sounds like whoever's behind this is one ruthless person," Mr. Drew said grimly. "Any suspects?"

"Two," Nancy replied. "Someone Paula knows at school and another exchange student. It's about time I check them both out."

Mr. Drew patted her shoulder. "Be extremely careful," he warned. "Make sure you call the police if you get in over your head."

"Don't worry," Nancy said, smiling. "I will."

"I'll be in my study if you need me."

After her father had left, Nancy finished the soup and ladled out another bowl. Then she reached for her purse and pulled out the charred letter she'd retrieved from the smoldering furniture.

She unfolded it carefully, but blackened bits still crumpled and fell into her lap. Sipping the soup, Nancy reread the letter.

"Inez, whose home is Essen, Germany, wishes to visit . . . Also, please remember to go to . . . drive

74

up to New York was . . . wishes to thank Pablo . . . will not be able to smoke . . ."

Nancy tossed the paper onto the table in frustration. What was so incriminating in the letter that Paula would want to burn it? Was there a hidden message or code? Had a note been scrawled on it somewhere?

Fishing through her purse, Nancy brought out her magnifying glass. She peered through it, scanning the page. Wait. There was a circle lightly penciled around the word *home.*

Nancy put down the magnifying glass. She couldn't see the circle with her naked eye. Picking it back up, she scanned the page again. There was another circle, and another.

Excitedly, Nancy grabbed a pencil from the holder next to the kitchen phone. Then she began jotting down the words, starting at the top of the page. There were four circled words in all. And when Nancy put them together, they revealed a chilling message:

Home . . . go . . . up . . . smoke!

9

Ticket to Trouble

Nancy folded the letter and put it on the table. The circled words in the newsletter had warned Paula about the fire at the Moorelys. So Paula had known about a possible fire before she arrived home. Did she also know or suspect who had set it? And if she did, why didn't she get help?

Unfolding the paper, Nancy studied the letter again. She wasn't quite sure how Paula had decoded it. Obviously, those four words weren't the entire message. Nancy guessed that Paula had been instructed to circle words at a certain interval. If Nancy hadn't witnessed the fire, "home . . . go . . . up . . . smoke" wouldn't have made much sense. The rest of the message must have been destroyed when the paper burned.

Excitedly, Nancy gulped down the rest of her soup. The newsletter had narrowed down her suspects. Neil from Ireland was the only person connected to the exchange program. It was still possible that Shaun or the guy in the ski jacket was somehow involved, though. She'd have to find out.

"555-6000," Nancy repeated the phone number. "Thanks, Mrs. Moorely. I'll call Mr. Taylor right away."

Nancy hung up the phone. It was Thursday, the morning following the fire. She was relieved to hear from Mrs. Moorely that the family was fine. They were staying at a hotel, but Nancy had been able to reach them at home, where they were sorting through the damaged items in the basement. They wouldn't be able to move back in until the whole house was repainted.

Nancy hoped she could reach Larry Taylor, the regional coordinator for the foreign student exchange program. Since it appeared that the newsletter had been used to send Paula a threatening message, Nancy assumed that someone from the program was involved. She wasn't sure what Mr. Taylor could tell her, but at this point any new information might be helpful.

She dialed Mr. Taylor's number, and he answered immediately.

"Hello, Mr. Taylor. I'm a friend of Suzanne Moorely and Paula de Jagger," Nancy said. "My family's interested in hosting an exchange student next year. I was wondering if you could give me some more information about your program."

"Why, certainly," the man said. "Would you like me to send you some brochures?"

"That'd be great." Nancy gave Mr. Taylor her address. "I also met Neil," she went on. "He's staying with the Chesters." Nancy hoped she sounded like an enthusiastic young girl. "He had such amazing things to say about your program that I couldn't wait to call."

"Oh, yes, Neil Galligan," Mr. Taylor said. Nancy quickly jotted down the Irish student's last name, and Mr. Taylor continued. She jumped at the chance when he invited her to a mid-year get-together, which the exchange program was throwing for all the foreign students and their host families.

"Sure! I'd love to come," Nancy said. "Friday night? I'll be there for sure. If my parents say it's okay, I mean. See you then."

She hung up and grinned. The call had been worthwhile after all. What a break, Nancy thought. Now she could finally meet Neil Galligan, the person to whom Paula was sending money. She might also find out if Shaun and the dark-haired boy were involved in the program.

Nancy checked her watch. Bess and Suzanne would be arriving any minute. Nancy had invited her friends for lunch. She hoped to get more information about Paula from Suzanne. And Bess had volunteered to spend the morning at Le Café, one of Paula's hangouts, and snoop around. She was going to report her findings to Nancy and Suzanne during lunch.

Nancy poked her head in the refrigerator and found yogurt, potato salad, a bag of Hannah's famous rolls, and cold cuts. They'd have quite a feast.

Bess burst through the back door just as Nancy finished setting out the food. "I'm starved," Bess said, throwing off her coat. She plunked down into a kitchen chair and reached for a chunk of cheese.

Nancy grinned. "Can't you at least wait until Suzanne gets here?"

"No way," Bess replied cheerfully. "Cold days like this make me absolutely ravenous."

"Didn't you just eat breakfast at Le Café?" Nancy asked.

Bess nodded. "Yep." Sneaking a slice of ham, she stuffed it in her mouth. "Croissants and an omelet." She took another slice of ham. "By the way, you owe me fifteen bucks."

Nancy gasped. "For breakfast?"

"Well, kind of." Bess leaned forward, a mysterious glint in her eyes. "I had to tip the waiter extra for a little information."

Nancy laughed. "I hope it was worth it, Private Eye Marvin."

"Well, the waiter told me Paula spends a lot of time there with some guy who rides a motorcycle and wears a leather jacket. I figured it had to be Shaun. Anyway, they were there last Friday and got into a big argument. The waiter thought it was about money."

"Good work, Bess," Nancy said. "That means we definitely need to find out more about Shaun Devane."

Just then, the doorbell rang.

79

"I'll answer it," Bess volunteered, reaching for a roll.

"Okay," Nancy said. "That'll give me time to put out more food."

Suzanne and Bess were chattering excitedly as they walked into the kitchen.

"Suzanne overheard part of a conversation Paula had this morning before school," Bess said. "And she thinks Paula was talking to Shaun."

Suzanne nodded. "She called him from the hotel room. I was fixing my hair in the bathroom, so I couldn't hear much. But she said something about more money."

"That ties in with what the waiter told me," Bess said.

Nancy frowned. "I thought Paula was paying off Neil. Maybe I was wrong."

"Shaun could easily be in on it, too," Suzanne said.

Nancy poured out three sodas. "Okay," she said. "When we drive Suzanne back to school after lunch, we'll find Shaun Devane. I think it's time we paid him a little visit."

"There he is," Suzanne whispered excitedly from the back seat. "Let's go get him." She reached for the door handle.

With a chuckle, Nancy stopped her. "This isn't a TV detective show, Suzanne. We don't 'get' anybody. Besides, look who's with him."

She nodded toward the school. Paula had just

walked out. She was running to catch up with Shaun.

"What's she carrying?" Bess asked.

"It looks like her guitar case," Suzanne said in a puzzled voice. "That's weird. She didn't say anything about needing it for school."

The girls watched as Shaun and Paula headed toward Shaun's motorcycle in the parking lot. Nancy tried to catch their expressions, but this time they were too far away.

When they reached the motorcycle, Shaun took Paula's guitar and strapped it onto the back.

"She must be going somewhere with him," Bess observed.

"And I bet it's not to work," Nancy added.

Shaun put his helmet on his head, then squeezed Paula's hand. She stepped back, and he climbed on his cycle. Then Paula turned and headed for the bus stop.

"It looks like she *is* going to work," Nancy said.

"So what's Shaun doing with her guitar?" Suzanne asked. "Paula brought it all the way from Holland."

"That's a good question." Nancy started the car. "Let's see if we can find out the answer."

She pulled away from the curb at the same time Shaun's motorcycle zoomed from the parking lot.

"You mean we're going to tail someone!" Suzanne exclaimed.

Nancy nodded. "You bet."

Suzanne settled back in her seat. "Okay," she

said. "But I hope I don't get caught for skipping classes. Maybe I should have my mother call the school and tell them I won't be in this afternoon."

Paula got on the bus, but Nancy stayed with Shaun until he steered onto the highway. Then she fell several cars behind. When he turned off, she expertly glided into his lane and made the same turn.

Nancy glanced at the street sign. Front Street was crowded with bars, and most of the stores were vacant. The ones that weren't had protective grilles covering the doors and windows. Broken bottles lay smashed along the curb, and trash blew in the wind.

"Yuck," Bess said as she peered out the window. "This isn't exactly the best part of town."

"Let's hope we don't have to get out of the car," Nancy said.

Nancy tailed Shaun for several blocks. Then he pulled into an empty parking space and stopped. Nancy cruised past and parked ahead of the motorcycle.

"Where do you think he's going?" Suzanne asked.

"Looks like that store right there." Bess pointed to a drab building with peeling paint and one window boarded up with plywood. As she'd predicted, Shaun went inside, carrying the guitar.

Nancy read the sign over the door to the others. "'Pete's Pawnshop. We take anything.'"

"Shaun's going to pawn Paula's guitar?" Suzanne asked.

"It looks like it." Nancy opened the car door. "But there's only one way to find out for sure."

"Don't you dare get out," Bess cried, grabbing Nancy's arm.

"I have to," Nancy said. "You two lock the doors. And don't worry, I'll stay in sight."

When she stepped outside, a blast of wind almost ripped off the car door. An old newspaper blew against Nancy's legs. Kicking it away, she turned up the collar of her coat and hurried to the front of the shop. The windows were so grimy that she could hardly see inside. Finally, Nancy found a crack between the window edge and the plywood. She peered through it nervously.

Shaun Devane and a tall man, probably Pete, were standing by a counter not far from the window. Shaun handed the man Paula's guitar. In return, the shopkeeper gave him a green ticket. It looked exactly like the one Nancy had found in Paula's leather handbag.

10

A Face in the Crowd

Nancy watched through the pawnshop window as Shaun pocketed the green ticket. Then, without even a nod, he spun around and headed for the door.

He was leaving! There was no way Nancy could make it back to the car in time.

Frantically, she looked around for a hiding place. There was a phone booth about ten feet down the sidewalk.

Nancy sprinted toward it. Ducking inside the booth, she pulled the door closed behind her. With a creak, it fell off one hinge and sagged precariously inward.

Nancy spun around at the same moment Shaun stepped out of the shop. She whipped the hood of her coat over her head and reached to pick up the receiver. All she could find was the silver cord it had once been attached to. Crooking her elbow,

Nancy held her hand under her hood next to her ear. Then she pretended to say hello.

Great, Nancy thought. If Shaun looks in the booth, he'll see some crazy girl trying to make a call on a busted phone.

She peeped out from under her hood as the blond boy marched past, his head down against the wind. His face was scrunched in a frown, and he glanced neither right nor left. Nancy thought Shaun looked like a person with a lot on his mind.

Only when his motorcycle disappeared around the corner did she dare venture out of the phone booth. By then, Bess and Suzanne were nervously peering out the car windows.

"You almost got caught," Bess said as she opened her car door. "What happened?"

Nancy told them about Shaun pawning Paula's guitar. "And the shop owner gave him a green claim ticket, just like the one I found in Paula's purse the other night."

"So she's pawned other things," Bess mused.

Nancy nodded. "Right. And I know a way to find out what else."

Bess groaned. "Why do I have the feeling this involves going into that sleazy shop?"

"I'll go!" Suzanne pushed past Bess and jumped out of the car. "Undercover work, right? It sounds exciting."

"I think safety in numbers is a good way to go," Nancy said. "Of course, you can always stay here, Bess. All alone in the car."

"No way." Bess quickly climbed out of the car,

clutching her purse tightly. Halfway up the sidewalk she called, "Are you guys coming?"

Nancy and Suzanne looked at each other and laughed. Then the two of them followed Bess into the pawnshop. It smelled like stale cigar smoke. When they got inside, the man behind the counter looked up.

"May I help you ladies?" he asked. Nancy noted the greedy expression in his eyes.

She looked at him innocently. "Well, I think so. The other day I brought something in here and, well . . . I . . ." She stumbled over her words and tried to look embarrassed. "I mean, I lost the ticket," she finally blurted out.

The man rolled his eyes and sighed. "Yeah. You and a hundred others."

"But I remember the number on the ticket," Nancy said with a bright smile.

Squinting, the man eyed her, then Bess and Suzanne. The two girls were standing like statues on either side of Nancy.

"Really, she did," Suzanne spoke up, her voice squeaking slightly. "I was with her."

"Then how come I don't remember you?" the guy sneered.

"We weren't dressed like this," Nancy said quickly. "We were . . . you know"—she flushed convincingly—"disguised."

"Yeah, yeah. Too embarrassed to be seen in here, but not too embarrassed to take my money."

The three girls nodded enthusiastically.

"All right. What's the number?"

"7846-MT." Nancy was glad she'd memorized the number on Paula's ticket.

The man sighed. "Wait here."

He slipped behind a curtain.

"Whew. That was quick thinking," Bess whispered.

Nancy put her fingers to her lips. "Shhh. He might have a camera on us."

He reappeared a few moments later, carrying a small box. "This is it."

"Thanks!" Nancy reached out to take the box, but the pawnshop owner snatched it away.

"Not so fast. That'll be four hundred bucks."

"Four hundred!" Nancy sputtered.

Leaning on the counter, the man smiled. His teeth were stained with tobacco.

"I know I only gave you three hundred, but the price has gone up since then." Opening the box, he pulled out two gold chains. One had a tulip pendant hanging from it.

When he dangled the necklace in front of Nancy, Suzanne gasped. Bess nudged her in the side.

"That's robbery," Nancy said.

With a shrug, the man dropped the necklaces back in the box. Nancy could see several other pieces of jewelry nestled in the bottom.

"You rich girls can always get plenty of dough," the store owner said.

Nancy gazed at him steadily. "Maybe. But how do I know you won't raise the price the next time we come in?"

"I won't. You've got my word."

Nancy glared at him, knowing he couldn't be trusted. Shaun couldn't be much of a friend if he'd led Paula to this sleazy guy. Then she remembered she was supposed to act sweet and naive.

"Okay," she said, sounding innocent. "We'll be back with four hundred dollars. Bye!" Then, linking her arms through Suzanne's and Bess's, she made a hasty exit.

Bess started coughing when they got outside. "Yuck. What a gross place."

"And what a snake." Suzanne made a face. "That was Paula's tulip necklace he had."

"I figured you recognized it," Nancy said. "What about the other one?"

Suzanne shook her head. "I've never seen her wear it."

"You don't think Paula stole the jewelry from the boutique, do you?" Bess halted in front of the car. "Maybe she pawned it at Pete's to get rid of it."

"Paula would never steal!" Suzanne rushed to her friend's rescue. "I know for sure that Ms. Hunt gave her the tulip necklace as payment for all her hard work.

"If you ask me, Shaun's the one we should be accusing," Suzanne continued huffily as she got in the car. "Right, Nancy?"

Nancy was silent as she turned the key in the ignition. "I don't know," she said finally. "Shaun's either an accomplice or he's helping Paula raise money. And I'm still not sure how the dark-haired guy fits in."

"Or where to find him," Bess added.

Nancy steered the car into the street. In a few minutes they were back on the highway.

"I'm hoping Paula can answer some of these questions," Nancy said.

"Then let's go to the mall and ask her," Suzanne said. "I want her to know she can count on us."

Nancy shook her head. "I don't think that's such a good idea. If we just show up out of the blue she might run." She checked her watch. "Unless we call first and tell her we want to take her to dinner again. An early one."

"Right. The one we owe her," Bess jumped in.

Suzanne's eyes glowed. "Good idea. Stop at the nearest phone booth. I'll call my mother, too, so she can excuse me from school."

Nancy laughed. "Let's hope the phone works better than the one outside Pete's Pawnshop."

"I don't get it," Suzanne said, glancing around the crowded mall. "Paula should be here by now."

"You did tell her five o'clock, right?" Nancy glanced at her watch.

Suzanne nodded. "Right. In front of the fountain."

"She's fifteen minutes late." Bess stood on tiptoe and scanned the crowd.

"Let's start walking toward Around the World," Nancy suggested. "Maybe Paula got held up."

"I'll stay here just in case she shows up while you're gone," Bess said, dropping onto a bench. She rubbed the heel of her foot. "These new shoes are killing me."

"Already?" Nancy shook her head in disbelief. "You just bought them."

Bess grimaced. "Well, they'll take a while to break in, I guess."

Nancy and Suzanne set off for the boutique. The store was crowded with customers. Nancy searched the small shop, but Paula was nowhere in sight. Finally, she caught Ms. Hunt's attention.

"Hi, girls," the store manager said, with a harried smile. "What can I do for you?"

"Paula was going to meet us for dinner at five," Suzanne said. "When she didn't show up, we thought she might still be working."

Ms. Hunt frowned. "That's odd. About four-thirty, she said she was feeling feverish. I told her to go home. She didn't look well at all when she left."

Suzanne and Nancy exchanged puzzled looks. They'd called around four-fifteen to make the dinner date.

"She couldn't—" Suzanne started to say.

Nancy squeezed her arm, trying to silence her. "Then I guess we'll catch her at home," she said quickly. "Thanks for your help."

Taking Suzanne by the elbow, she abruptly steered her from the store.

"But when I called Paula, she sounded great," Suzanne protested when they were outside. "She couldn't have gotten sick in fifteen minutes."

"You're right," Nancy agreed. "But Paula wants Ms. Hunt to think she's sick."

"But what could have happened?"

"I'm not sure." Nancy frowned. "My guess is

90

something happened that scared her. Either that, or she's avoiding us."

Nancy hurried toward the escalator. "Let's get Bess and go to your hotel. Maybe Paula did head back there."

Suddenly Nancy stopped dead in her tracks. Standing ten feet away was the dark-haired guy in the blue ski jacket. He was scanning the crowd, obviously searching for someone. This time, Nancy wasn't going to let him get away.

"Suzanne," she hissed. "Stay here."

Slowly, Nancy walked closer, her face turned toward the display windows as if she was an eager shopper. She could see the dark-haired boy's reflection in the glass. When she was opposite him, she looked down and pretended to rummage in her purse. Then, with two quick strides, she was standing next to him.

Shooting out her hand, Nancy grabbed his wrist.

"Hello," she said quietly. "I know you're a friend of Paula's."

His face flushed angrily. Stepping backward, he tried to pull away. Nancy held his wrist tighter.

"Look, if you're a friend of Paula's, you don't have anything to worry about. But if you're not, I'm calling security," she bluffed.

The boy tensed. Nancy studied him. He had wavy black hair and piercing green eyes. His full mouth was set in a grim line.

For a moment, she could feel him almost relax. Maybe he was going to trust her.

"Did you get him? Is he the blackmailer?"

Suzanne rushed toward them, waving her arms excitedly.

Nancy twisted around to hush her at the same instant the boy jerked his arm from her grasp. In an instant, he was free and running for the escalator.

Nancy sprinted after him. He jumped onto the top step just as she reached him.

"Wait!" She grabbed for his coat and held on.

The moving steps pulled her onto the escalator. Angrily, the young man yanked his coat from her hand. Nancy lost her balance. With a sharp cry, she pitched forward, past the boy and down the steep metal steps.

11

Deadly Words

At the last second, a strong arm circled Nancy's waist. It jerked her backward, stopping her fall. Doubling over, Nancy gasped, the wind knocked out of her. Then her feet found a step, and she regained her balance.

"Thanks," she wheezed, turning to the guy in the ski jacket.

He dropped his arm from around her waist. In one swift move, he vaulted the side of the still-moving escalator and raced toward the exit.

"No!" Nancy yelled. She couldn't believe he was getting away.

Nancy took off down the escalator, jumping the last steps to the first floor of the mall. She started for the exit, but a stitch of pain pierced her side. With a cry, she stopped short.

The dark-haired boy had disappeared out the

mall doors and into the parking lot. She'd lost him again.

"I can't believe it," Nancy said aloud. Her breath was coming in ragged gasps. She sat down on the edge of the fountain and rubbed her bruised ribs. Thank goodness that was all that hurt. If she'd fallen down those steep steps . . . She shuddered to think what might have happened.

"Nancy!" Suzanne waved from the escalator. "Are you all right?"

Without looking up, Nancy nodded.

"What an awesome save." Suzanne chattered excitedly as she hopped off the escalator. "Like a scene from a movie. No, better than a scene from a movie. I mean, that guy kept you from plunging twenty feet to your—"

"Suzanne," Nancy interrupted, "this isn't a movie."

"Oh, right." Suzanne shut her mouth and sat down. "I blew it back there, didn't I?"

"Forget it." Nancy grinned.

Just then, Bess limped up on her new shoes. "So there you guys are," she said. "What took you so long?"

Nancy and Suzanne looked at each other. Then they both began to giggle.

"O-o-oh." Nancy grimaced and held her side. "Don't make me laugh. Come on," she said, standing up. "We'd better go to the hotel and see if we can find Paula."

"Then we should try our house. My mom's there with the painters," Suzanne added.

As the girls walked out to the car, Nancy filled Bess in on the encounter with the dark-haired boy. Suzanne told her about Paula telling Ms. Hunt she was going home sick.

At the hotel fifteen minutes later Suzanne checked the Moorelys' rooms.

"There's no sign that Paula's been there since this morning," Suzanne reported as she climbed back into Nancy's car.

Paula wasn't at the Moorelys' house, either. Nancy looked around. Canvas tarps covered the furniture in the living room, and everything smelled of new paint.

"Paula came by around five, picked up a few things, and asked me if she could spend the night at Amy's house," Mrs. Moorely explained. Amy was the head cheerleader and Paula's close friend. "She said something about a surprise party they were planning."

Bess, Suzanne, and Nancy exchanged dubious looks.

"Oh, no." Mrs. Moorely put a hand to her mouth. "Do you think she made that all up?"

"Did Amy come and get her?" Nancy asked.

Mrs. Moorely shook her head. "Paula said she'd take the bus."

"Let's call Amy's house," Suzanne said.

"Good thinking," Nancy said. "Something tells me Paula's not there."

While Suzanne used the hall phone, Nancy and Bess filled Mrs. Moorely in on their trip to the pawnshop and their adventure at the mall.

"I hope there's some simple explanation for all this." Mrs. Moorely wrung her hands.

Suzanne hung up the phone. "She's not there," she said in a worried voice. "And Amy didn't know anything about planning a surprise party."

"I should have known something was wrong," Mrs. Moorely said with a sigh.

"Let's start calling around," Nancy suggested.

Suzanne got out the phone book, and the girls took turns calling Paula's friends. None of them had seen Paula.

"She must be hiding from someone," Bess said.

"I bet it's the guy at the mall," Suzanne said. "He looked dangerous."

"I think we'd better call the police," Mrs. Moorely said, reaching for the phone. "This has gone far enough."

"Wait," Nancy said. "The police won't do anything unless someone's been missing for twenty-four hours. We'll just have to hope Paula's safe for the night. If she doesn't show up tomorrow, we can alert the police."

"But where could she be?" Suzanne wailed.

Nancy shook her head. "I don't know. But she obviously doesn't trust anyone—including us."

Nancy called Suzanne on Friday afternoon. Suzanne had already phoned once from school to tell her that Paula hadn't shown up.

Now Suzanne was really worried. "My mom called the police," she told Nancy. "They said

Paula will probably come home on her own, but they took her name and a description."

"Good," Nancy said. "That big party for all the exchange students is tonight. Let's hope she'll show up there. In the meantime, we can make some more calls."

"Why don't you come over?" Suzanne suggested. "We've moved back in. It smells like paint, but you can't even tell there was a fire."

"All right," Nancy said. "I'll pick up Bess and be right over. I'd like to look through Paula's room, if that's okay with you. There might be some clue there about where she went."

Nancy hung up and phoned Bess. Her friend was eager to help.

Fifteen minutes later, they were at the Moorelys' house.

"I already called the boutique," Suzanne said when she opened the front door. "Ms. Hunt hasn't seen her since yesterday. But Paula had already arranged to have the night off because of the party."

"Which starts in two hours," Nancy said. "We'll have to work fast."

"Who should we call next?" Bess picked up the phone receiver.

"Let's try the cheerleaders again," Suzanne suggested.

For the next half hour, the girls talked to Paula's friends. Still, no one had seen the exchange student.

Bess slumped in a chair. "Looks like we're at a dead end."

"Not yet." Nancy started for the stairs. "There's still Paula's room. Coming, Suzanne?"

Suzanne smiled with glee. "Sure. I've always wanted to snoop through her things."

"This is not snooping," Nancy corrected. "We're trying to find something that will help us track down Paula. She may be in danger."

"Oh, right." Suzanne's smile turned serious.

Bess picked up the phone book again. "While you're doing that, I'll try these last two names on the list."

Nancy and Suzanne went upstairs and into Paula's room. For a moment, Nancy stood with her hands on her hips and surveyed the room. There was a closet filled with clothes, a small wooden desk, an unmade bed, and a dresser with several framed pictures on top.

"Where should we start?" Suzanne asked.

"I wish I knew," Nancy answered. "Let's check and see if there's another coded newsletter around. In fact, look for any correspondence from the exchange program."

Suzanne nodded and headed for Paula's desk. Nancy took the dresser.

Picking up a picture in a ceramic frame, she studied it curiously. An attractive man and woman with a tow-headed boy smiled from the photo. Nancy guessed they were Paula's family. The other pictures showed Paula with kids her own age. There was no one who looked like the dark-haired guy in the ski jacket, so Nancy had to assume he wasn't a friend from the Netherlands.

Next Nancy checked between the photos and the frames for anything hidden there. Finding nothing, she set the pictures back on the dresser. A careful search of the dresser drawers revealed nothing unusual.

Nancy straightened. She noticed Suzanne had been awfully quiet as she searched. The redhead was sitting in the desk chair, reading a letter.

"Did you find anything?" Nancy asked.

"Huh?" Suzanne dropped the letter and looked up with a guilty smile. "Uh, no. I mean, I can't make out all of it, but it looks like a letter from some guy in Amsterdam." She blushed.

"Suzanne. We're hunting for *clues*," Nancy reminded her.

"Right, right." Suzanne began busily leafing through a stack of books.

Nancy decided to tackle the closet. Standing on tiptoe, she rummaged through the shoeboxes and piles of sweaters on the closet shelf. Then she dropped to her knees. Paula's luggage was pushed toward the back.

Nancy opened the suitcases and ran her fingers into every fold and under every flap. Nothing. Frustrated, she sat back on her heels.

If she were Paula, where would she hide something a blackmailer might want?

Her gaze settled on a pair of fleece-lined suede boots. She felt inside, and her fingers touched a

99

piece of paper. Excitedly, she pulled it out and unfolded it. It was a copy of a document written in Dutch. The postmark on the envelope was dated Monday.

"Suzanne!" Nancy jumped to her feet. "Do you have a Dutch-English dictionary?"

Suzanne nodded, then ran out of the room.

Nancy scanned the document. A word in bold writing at the top of the form leaped out at her: *Politie.* Could the word be "Police"?

"Here." Suzanne thrust the pocket-sized dictionary into Nancy's hand. Ten minutes later, the two girls had translated enough to discover that Paula had once been picked up for shoplifting.

"Shoplifting," Nancy whispered to herself. Her mind flew back to the day Paula had caught the shoplifter. Could there possibly be a link between Paula and the girl she'd caught?

Suzanne pointed to the document. "Do you think this is what the blackmailer has on Paula? I mean, it's not like she went to jail or anything."

Nancy shook her head, afraid to reveal her thoughts to Suzanne. If she was right and Paula was involved in another shoplifting scheme, then the exchange student was in big trouble.

Bess came into the room. "Sorry I took so long. No luck. What did you guys find?"

Suzanne showed her the document and their translation. While the two of them chattered away, Nancy went over to the desk. Suzanne had been so engrossed in the love letters, she might have missed something.

Opening each book, Nancy held them page down and shook them. Two papers fluttered from the third book. They were newsletters from the exchange program.

Nancy skimmed over them. She could make out a few very faint penciled circles on the second one.

She took the page over to the window and held it up to the light. "Yes!" she exclaimed.

Nancy ripped a piece of paper from a school notebook and jotted down the circled words. "You're . . . behind . . . in . . . your . . . obligation . . . interest . . . rising."

She checked the date at the top. The newsletter was for November 7. That was the same month Suzanne had noticed a big change in Paula. Obviously, someone had been putting pressure on her.

The second newsletter was dated January 15. That's today's date, Nancy said to herself, noticing that no words were circled.

Nancy went back to the first paper. Quickly, she counted the intervals between the words. Paula had circled every sixth word in the third paragraph.

Picking up the latest newsletter, Nancy tried the formula on the first paragraph and circled every sixth word. Send . . . kids . . . Sheila . . . on . . . know . . . address.

It didn't make sense. If there was a message, Nancy realized, it had to be located in a specific paragraph. But which one?

Grabbing her purse off the bed, Nancy took out the burned newsletter she'd retrieved at the fire. She checked the date on the top. January 10. Two newsletters sent within a week. The blackmailer was getting impatient.

Nancy took a wild guess. Since the messages in the two previous letters had first used the third paragraph, then the fourth paragraph, maybe she should try the fifth paragraph in the latest letter.

Skimming the paper, Nancy quickly underlined every sixth word as she read the paragraph.

"Don't forget to write down *this* date—January 16th, which is *Saturday*. The exchange program hosts its *last* party. This will be your *chance* to meet new friends and *be* reunited with old. So be *there!* Larry Taylor will call you *or* write everyone with details or *else* you'll be contacted via a friend."

Quickly, Nancy wrote down the underlined words, then read them out loud.

"This . . . Saturday . . . last . . . chance . . . be . . . there . . . or . . . else."

12

The Party Connection

No wonder Paula had panicked, Nancy thought. Something was going to happen Saturday—only a day away.

"Nan?" Bess shook Nancy's shoulder. "Are you all right? I've called you three times."

"What?" Nancy focused on Bess's face.

"You look like you're off on another planet," Suzanne said.

Bess frowned. "Or she's figured out something she doesn't like."

Nancy showed her friends the message.

Bess gasped. "That's tomorrow!"

Nancy nodded.

"What do you think it means?" Suzanne asked, her voice almost a whisper.

"I think it has something to do with a shoplifting scheme," Nancy said quietly.

"What?" Suzanne cried.

"It's just a hunch," Nancy said. She held up the police report from the Netherlands. "Someone obviously sent this to scare Paula. Maybe they don't want just money anymore."

"But Paula would never steal anything," Suzanne insisted.

"Unless she was forced to," Nancy said. "And whoever's behind this scheme is pretty ruthless. They already set fire to your house. That means they'll stop at nothing to get what they want."

"But who?" Suzanne asked.

"I wish I knew." Nancy clenched her fists. "Maybe we'll find out at the party tonight."

"Do you think Neil Galligan or Shaun Devane might show up?" Bess asked.

"Or maybe our mystery man at the mall," Nancy replied, checking her watch. "Wow! It's almost seven-thirty." Grabbing her purse, Nancy headed out the door. "Come on, Bess. I'll drop you off."

"Hey! Where are you rushing off to?" Suzanne called down the hall.

"I have to get ready for a party," Nancy called back over her shoulder. "And so do you! I'll pick you up in forty-five minutes."

Nancy was slipping her black suede flats onto her stockinged feet when the doorbell rang.

"I'll get it!" she called to her dad, who was in his study. Grabbing her purse, she flew down the stairs to the hall.

When she opened the front door, a tall, dark-haired man greeted her with a friendly smile. He was wearing a long tweed overcoat. A manila envelope was tucked under his arm.

"Nancy Drew? I'm Larry Taylor, coordinator of the foreign student exchange program."

"Oh, hi." Nancy stepped aside and ushered him into the hall. A blast of cold night air followed him inside. "I was expecting to see you at the party," she added.

"I realize that," Mr. Taylor said, nodding. "But I had to pass this way to get to the party, so I thought I'd drop off the information about the program in person." He smiled cordially. "I was afraid I'd be so busy hosting the party, I wouldn't have a chance to give you the packet, much less talk to you." He handed Nancy the envelope.

"Well, thanks," she said. "Would you like to sit down?"

Mr. Taylor waved away her offer. "Oh, no. I can't stay. I need to be at the party early. I'm anxious to see my students. It's been at least a month. Thank heavens they're all doing so well. They're a good bunch of kids."

"Even Paula de Jagger?" Nancy blurted out.

The coordinator's brow furrowed in confusion. "I'm not quite sure what you mean. I hope there hasn't been any trouble."

"No," Nancy quickly reassured him. "Except . . ." She hesitated. Should she confide in Mr. Taylor? Paula might even have contacted him for help. She glanced up at the tall man. He was watching her with genuine concern.

"Except I'm afraid Paula might not be at the party," Nancy said finally. "She's disappeared."

"What?" he exclaimed, looking alarmed. "Why didn't someone call me?"

"Because we're not sure what's happened. The Moorelys contacted the police, and they suggested we wait. Do you have any idea where she might be?"

Larry Taylor shook his head. "No. But I do remember Mrs. Moorely calling me with some concerns."

"Right. You told her Paula was probably homesick," Nancy said.

Sighing, the man rubbed the bridge of his nose. Nancy felt guilty about springing the news on him right before the party.

"I hope nothing's happened." He shook his head worriedly. "Paula's too levelheaded to do something stupid."

"Is there anything you can tell the Moorelys that might help them find her?" Nancy asked.

Mr. Taylor thought for a moment. "I'll have to check my files, but it seems I remember something about cousins in California. But why would she go there without telling anyone?" His eyes bored into Nancy's. "Is Paula in some kind of trouble?"

Bending down, Nancy pretended to fix her stocking. The coordinator obviously knew she wasn't telling him everything.

And why should she? If Paula didn't trust anyone, then Nancy knew she should be careful, too.

Taking a deep breath, Nancy straightened. "I

don't know," she said truthfully. "I was hoping you might have the answer."

"I wish I did." Mr. Taylor sighed. "The last time I talked to Paula she seemed really happy." He checked his watch. "I have a few minutes. Maybe I should drive over and talk to the Moorelys."

Nancy nodded. "I'm sure they'd appreciate it. They were going to contact you soon, anyway. Do you need directions to their house?" she offered.

"No, no, I was just there in August. Even at night, that bright yellow house will be easy to spot." He held out his hand. "It was nice meeting you, Ms. Drew," he said with a warm smile.

"I'll see you at the party." Nancy shook Mr. Taylor's hand, then opened the door.

He paused before stepping out. "Let's hope that Paula will be there, too," he said.

"Now, Suzanne," Nancy warned, "all I want you to do at the party is keep your eyes and ears open. Then report back to me—quietly."

"That sounds boring," Suzanne complained as they pulled into the parking lot of Le Café.

"But safe." Nancy turned off the motor and peered out the frosty window. The parking lot was packed with cars. Nancy had been to the restaurant only once before, the previous summer. She and Bess had eaten on a sunny terrace overlooking a small lake. Now the terrace and tables were covered with snow.

"Besides, you have an important job," Nancy reminded Suzanne.

Suzanne sighed. "I know. Find out who Neil Galligan is."

"Right," Nancy said. "Also, we need to see if Shaun or the guy in the ski jacket is here. I'm betting one of them is involved with the exchange program or someone in it. And," she added in a quiet voice, "we need to find Paula."

"What if she's not here?" Suzanne asked. The parking lot lights cast deep shadows around her eyes.

Nancy touched her hand. "Then we'll just have to keep looking."

The two girls got out of the car. A brisk wind blew Nancy's hair in a swirl. She was glad she'd worn her long goosedown coat.

Le Café was toasty warm. A fire roared in the center of a large, table-filled room. Plants and baskets hung from the ceiling. A few diners were talking over coffee. Nancy could hear laughter from another room around the corner. She and Suzanne hung up their coats in the entranceway, then headed for the private room that had been rented for the party.

Nancy nervously squeezed her palms together. When she stepped into the doorway, she surveyed the room quickly. Her heart sank.

"She's not here," Suzanne whispered, looking disappointed.

"Not yet," Nancy said. "Now come on, smile. This is a party. Let's split up and talk to people."

Suzanne forced a smile, then waved at a girl on the other side of the room. Nancy went over to the refreshment table. She didn't see Larry Taylor and figured he was still at the Moorelys'.

"Hi! How about a glass of punch or some cookies?" a cheerful voice said at her elbow.

Nancy turned to see a heavyset girl with sparkling blue eyes holding out a paper cup.

"Dip? Chips? Cupcakes?" She giggled. "I'm in charge of refreshments, so I don't want anyone to go hungry."

"Thanks. I'd love some." Nancy helped herself to a gooey-looking brownie.

"Everyone's talking so much, they're not really eating," the girl confided. She was munching on a carrot stick. "I'm Ellen."

"Hi, I'm Nancy. Are you sponsoring an exchange student?"

"Yes." She pointed across the room. "The tall girl over there with the long brown hair. Angelina from Portugal. What about you?"

"Nope. I'm a friend of Paula de Jagger."

Ellen raised her eyebrows. "Where is Paula tonight? She's coming, isn't she?"

"Oh, she's running late," Nancy said. "Hey, have you seen Neil Galligan lately?"

"Ooo, that handsome Irish guy?" Ellen giggled. "Yeah. We saw him at a party two weeks ago."

Nancy took a wild chance. Lowering her voice, she said, "I heard he dyed his hair green and got a really short haircut and blue contact lenses."

"Neil? Never. All the girls love that wavy black hair and those gorgeous green eyes."

Nancy practically dropped her plate on the floor.

"And was he wearing that same blue ski jacket?" she asked carefully.

Ellen nodded. "He never takes it off."

Wavy black hair. Green eyes. Neil Galligan and the mystery guy at the mall had to be the same person!

13

One Wrong Step

"All right!" Nancy exclaimed. Her hunch had been right on target. But Ellen was looking at her curiously. "I mean, thank goodness Neil still looks the same," Nancy added quickly.

"Hey, don't you want more to eat?" Ellen asked as Nancy spun around to look for Suzanne.

"I'll get another brownie later," Nancy said over her shoulder. "Nice to meet you."

Nancy started fitting the pieces of the puzzle together. Neil Galligan might have roped Paula into last Monday's shoplifting scheme. Maybe Paula was supposed to open the case so the other girl could take the jewelry. Neil had been outside the boutique, probably making sure that everything went according to plan. But when Paula caught the shoplifter instead of letting her get away, Neil was probably furious. That's when he'd called the Moorelys with the threat.

And Neil might have been the one who set the fire. That would explain why he'd bolted in his car when she'd confronted him.

Then Paula must have seen Neil at the mall the previous day, too. That was why she'd run away instead of meeting Nancy and the others for dinner.

If Neil was the blackmailer, he was going to force Paula to do something Saturday. But what? Nancy wondered. Another shoplifting scheme?

As Nancy started toward the ladies' room, a face peered in the front window of the restaurant. Nancy's heart flew into her throat. It was Neil Galligan! His green eyes locked on hers.

Nancy darted for the front door and swung it open. A blast of icy air stung her cheeks. She glimpsed a flash of Neil's blue ski jacket as he disappeared around the other side of the restaurant.

Without hesitation, Nancy raced after him. She turned the corner and ran onto the snow-covered terrace. Then she stopped, her breath blowing from her mouth in frosty gasps. Where had he gone?

A confusing path of tracks led across the dimly lit terrace. He's smart, Nancy thought. He's following someone else's trail.

She shivered. She knew she was crazy to stay out in the cold without her coat. But if she went back inside to get it, she'd lose Neil for sure.

Slipping and sliding in her flat pumps, Nancy wound her way past the empty iron tables to the other side of the terrace. The moonlight cast eerie shadows on the blanket of snow.

Nancy couldn't see Neil anywhere, but she did spot tracks leading down the slope to the lake. Stepping in the footprints, she made her way down a slippery bank. The howling wind cut through her dress as if it weren't there, and the snow soaked through her shoes and stung her feet with the icy cold.

The trail stopped on the shore of the tree-lined lake. Nancy searched the hard ground, her teeth chattering. If Neil had gone along the frozen bank, she wouldn't see his tracks. But what about the lake? Nancy checked the glistening ice. It didn't look thick enough to hold a person. Nancy guessed that Neil had stayed on the shore and disappeared into the trees somewhere.

Suddenly, two hands shoved her hard in the back. Nancy flew forward. With a cry, she threw her arms over her face to protect it.

Whack! Nancy landed hard on the ice. For a moment, she lay still, feeling dazed and bruised. Then the biting cold jolted her to her senses.

Catching her breath, Nancy pushed herself up on her hands. Her body ached from the fall, but nothing felt broken. She looked behind her. The force of the push had propelled her about ten feet from the shore.

With small sliding movements, Nancy inched backward on her hands and knees. *Crack!* The sound shot a shiver of terror through Nancy's rigid body. The ice was cracking beneath her! She froze, her heart racing.

Cold water was seeping through a break in the

ice, washing over her numb fingers. Turning her head, Nancy yelled for help, but the wind whisked her cry into the night sky. There was no way anyone would hear her.

Don't panic, Nancy told herself. Lie flat and slide yourself toward shore.

Slowly, Nancy lowered herself onto her stomach on the wet ice. Then, cautiously, she began to worm her way backward.

Crack! She could feel the ice split beneath her thigh. More water washed over her leg.

Tears stung Nancy's eyes. Don't give up, a voice said inside her. But I'm so cold! she told the voice.

"Grab this!"

Nancy frowned. Had someone said something?

"Grab my coat sleeve."

Slowly, she raised her head. Someone was waving from the shore. The person lay down across the ice and tossed a jacket toward her. The end of one sleeve landed about a foot from Nancy. The other sleeve was in the person's hand.

"Hurry!" The male voice was loud and urgent. Stretching her arm as far as she could, Nancy reached for the leather sleeve.

"Now hold on."

Nancy grabbed the sleeve and clung with all her might. Her fingers were so numb they ached. Inch by inch, her rescuer dragged Nancy across the ice. When she was several feet from land, he stood up and lifted her onto the shore.

Nancy slumped to the ground, shaking. The

114

jacket was thrown over her shoulders. Nancy peered into the person's face.

It was Shaun Devane.

Her eyes widened in surprise.

"Do you think anything's frostbitten?" he asked.

She shook her head.

"Then you have to get up and walk."

Nancy laughed weakly. "Are you kidding? I can't even feel my legs."

"You have to," Shaun commanded. His strong arms pulled her to her feet. "You've got to get your blood circulating."

Nancy took one step, then another. Her legs began to tingle. Soon she could actually feel her feet again.

"Let's get you inside," Shaun said, helping her up the slope.

When they reached the terrace, Nancy stopped to catch her breath.

"Thanks," she said, smiling thinly. "If you hadn't come along, I don't know what I would have done." Then she paused. "How did you know I was down there?" she asked, hoping he didn't notice the suspicion in her voice.

Shaun shrugged. "I was just getting out of my car when I heard you yell for help."

Nancy held the jacket tighter around her. "What are you doing here?"

He laughed. "You almost froze to death, and you're still asking questions. Paula told me you're a hotshot detective."

"You're avoiding my question," Nancy said.

"I'll answer it as soon as you get inside, okay?" Shaun replied.

Nancy's teeth were still chattering. "Good enough," she said. "A cup of hot chocolate would be good, too."

Shaun held her elbow as they crossed the terrace. Once inside, Nancy got her own coat and purse and headed for the ladies' room. She saw in the mirror that the front of her dress was soaked. Stepping into a booth, she slid the dress over her head, then took off her stockings.

She dried herself as best she could with paper towels and put her dress back on. Then she stood in front of the hand dryer and let the hot air blow on her. She was still a little cold and clammy, but when she wrapped her long goosedown coat around her, she felt warmer.

When Nancy came out, Shaun was waiting with a steaming mug of hot chocolate.

"Wow. Thanks twice." Nancy held the mug with both hands and took a sip. "Mmm. Okay, so how about that answer to my question?"

"Only if you answer a question for me." Shaun shoved his hands in his jeans pockets.

Nancy studied him closely. With raised brows, he studied her. Both of them refused to look away.

It was hard to tell whose side Shaun Devane was on. He might be behind Paula's disappearance, or he could be working with Neil. But if Nancy didn't get him talking, she'd never find out.

"It's a deal," she said finally, sitting down at a

116

small table in a dark corner of the restaurant. The sound of loud voices told her that the party was still going strong in the private room.

Shaun sat opposite Nancy, facing the door to the party room. "I'm here because Paula invited me. I was supposed to be her date for the party."

"So where is she?" Nancy asked.

"That's the question I was going to ask you," he said. "But I have another question. What were you doing in the middle of the lake?"

"I was pushed," Nancy said flatly.

Shaun looked puzzled. "What do you mean? Who pushed you?"

"I'm not sure." Nancy watched his face, trying to detect a reaction. Shaun could have been the one who pushed her, thinking that if he conveniently "rescued" her, she wouldn't suspect he was involved in the blackmailing.

"Is the person who pushed you tied up somehow with why Paula's not here?" he asked, his eyes narrowing.

Nancy paused, wondering how much Shaun knew. She wanted to find out without revealing too much. But to do that, she'd have to take a chance. "I think so," she answered. "If I'm right, Paula's being blackmailed."

Shaun sucked in his breath.

"You obviously guessed something like that was going on." Nancy continued to watch his face for a reaction.

"Yeah." Shaun tossed down the last of his drink and slammed the glass on the table.

"I also know that the fire at the Moorelys' house was set," Nancy said.

"You seem to know a lot," Shaun scowled. Suddenly, without warning, he leaned forward, grasped Nancy's wrist, and pulled her down by the side of the table.

"What——?" Nancy began.

"Quiet!" Shaun commanded. Reaching over with his other hand, he pushed Nancy's head beneath the table.

Too late, Nancy realized that she'd played her hunch all wrong.

Shaun was guilty, too. And probably very dangerous.

14

A Dangerous Rendezvous

Nancy tried to twist free from Shaun's strong grasp, but the blond-haired boy only held her tighter. She heard the restaurant door open, then footsteps move swiftly across the floor. Someone was coming toward them.

"Help!" she gasped, but Shaun covered her mouth with his hand, and she knew no one would hear her.

"Shhh," Shaun said. When the footsteps died away, he slowly removed his hand.

"Sorry," he apologized sheepishly. "Hope I didn't hurt you."

What? Why was Shaun Devane suddenly acting nice?

"What on earth is going on?" Nancy demanded, glaring at him. She raised her head and banged it on the table. Grimacing, Nancy rubbed her head. "I thought you were going to do me in!"

Shaun snorted. "Do you in? I was trying to protect you." He nodded toward the private room. "I think the person who just walked in might be Paula's blackmailer."

"Where?" Nancy spun around in her seat.

"He went into the party." Shaun caught her hand when Nancy started to get up. "Wait a minute. Don't go running in there. If he sees you, we'll lose him."

"Who is it?" Nancy asked.

Shaun shook his head. "I don't know his name. He's a tall, dark-haired guy."

Nancy caught her breath. "Neil Galligan, I bet. He must think I'm at the bottom of the lake by now." She looked back up at Shaun. "So what makes you think this guy's involved?"

Shaun shrugged. "I followed Paula one night when she seemed really upset. She met the guy at a truck stop diner outside of town. I watched from the parking lot. They had a big argument." He grinned. "I was about to rush in like a knight in shining armor when the guy split."

"When was that?" Nancy asked.

"Monday night," Shaun replied. "Anyway, I went in and confronted Paula about it, but she wouldn't tell me anything. So I just took her home. Even though it was snowing, she had me drop her off about a block away from her house."

"That's the same night I caught her trying to sneak into the Moorelys'," Nancy said. "Is there anything else you can tell me that might help?"

The blond boy hesitated.

"Look." Propping her elbows on the table, Nancy leaned toward him. "If Neil's here, he must be looking for Paula. If he finds her, I think he's going to force her to do something dangerous. We need to find her before she gets hurt. There might not be much time."

Shaun's eyes flashed angrily. "I was afraid something like this was happening. But Paula wouldn't tell me anything." He banged the table with his fist.

"You helped her raise money to pay him off, didn't you?" Nancy asked.

Shaun nodded. "Yeah. She fed me this story about a sick friend back in the Netherlands. But I could see Paula was scared. You were right to suspect me that day in the alley. I was following the bus Paula took—although I took a detour so Paula wouldn't know—then I got back on the bus route and found her near the post office. I was furious because she wouldn't let me help her." He sighed. "It's only because I care. Paula's helped me a lot this year. I wasn't the world's best student, but she had faith in me."

He sounded sincere to Nancy. "Don't worry," she said. "I'll find her."

"*We'll* find her," Shaun corrected. "And I think I know just the place to look. We can take my car." He grabbed his jacket off the back of the seat and stood up.

Nancy quickly finished her hot chocolate and followed him out the door. She decided not to tell

Suzanne where she was going. The evening might get tricky, and she didn't need an overzealous "private eye" messing things up.

Quickly, Nancy wrote Suzanne a note on a napkin telling her she'd left and to get a ride home. She handed the note to a waiter, and she and Shaun slipped quietly away.

Shaun pointed to a beat-up white sports car parked outside. "It was too cold for the bike tonight," he told Nancy. "Anyway, if my hunch is right," he said as they climbed in, "Paula's at the same truck stop."

"But wouldn't that be the first place Neil would look?" Nancy said doubtfully.

"Maybe not," Shaun replied. "If he thinks Paula's hiding from him, he's going to be checking out her friends." Shaun pulled the sports car onto the highway.

Nancy studied Shaun in the light from the dashboard. His jaw was clenched, and his hands gripped the steering wheel so tightly that his knuckles were white.

It suddenly occurred to Nancy that she hadn't told anyone where she was going. And no one had seen the two of them together. If Shaun was working with Neil, he could be leading her right into a trap. She'd definitely have to stay on her toes.

They reached the truck stop about half an hour later. "Let's just hope Paula's here," Shaun said grimly. He took a left, and they cruised past the large, brightly lit windows of a diner. Nancy could see most of the booths inside.

"There she is!" she cried, pointing to the back of the restaurant. A blond-haired girl was sitting alone in a booth, hunched over a plate of food. Nancy recognized Paula's long braid.

But just as Shaun pulled into a parking spot, a red car raced past them. With a squeal of tires, it came to a stop in front of the diner entrance. Neil jumped out.

"That's him! Galligan!" Nancy scrambled from the car, but she was too far away to catch up to him. He was up the steps and had slammed the door in no time.

"Did he see you?" Shaun asked anxiously as he came around to Nancy's side.

"No," Nancy replied. "But obviously we were wrong. He's checking out their meeting place."

Shaun slammed his fist into his palm. "Let's give him a surprise he won't forget."

Nancy put a hand on his arm. "Take it easy," she cautioned. "We don't want to put Paula in any more danger than she already is in. Let's watch a minute and see what happens."

As she and Shaun crossed the pavement to the steps, Nancy kept her eye on Paula through the window. Neil was walking toward Paula.

Suddenly, Shaun stopped halfway up the walk, his gaze directed toward Neil. "Hey, wait a minute. That's not the guy I saw Paula with that night."

"It's not?" Nancy stared at Shaun in surprise, then back into the restaurant. Paula was gesturing to Neil to join her in the booth. The blond girl looked happy to see him.

123

Nancy frowned. What was going on? She'd been positive that Neil was the blackmailer. But if she was right, then why was Paula looking so happy?

She watched as Neil greeted Paula and sat down opposite her in the booth. Soon the two of them were deep in conversation.

Nancy touched Shaun's sleeve lightly. "Let's go in. I don't want to scare Paula off, though, so follow my lead."

Hardly anyone looked up when they entered the restaurant. Nancy huddled over a glass counter, her back to Paula. She pretended to study the array of gum and candy, but her real focus was on the wall mirror behind the counter.

In a few moments, Nancy took in the length of the diner. "There's an adjoining booth on the other side of Neil and Paula's," she whispered to Shaun. "It has a high partition. If we're really quiet, they probably won't see us sit down."

Shaun nodded and followed Nancy down the aisle. The two of them slid quietly onto the benches. The high partition kept Nancy from seeing Neil and Paula, but she could still hear snatches of their conversation.

As she listened, she picked up a menu and pretended to study it.

". . . can't take it anymore . . ."

". . . no more blackmailing . . ."

". . . fire was the last straw . . ."

". . . got to get him so he can't do this to anyone else!"

Slowly, Nancy put down the menu. Neil and

Paula were definitely talking about a third person, who had to be the blackmailer. But Nancy had been so sure the blackmailer was Neil. And Shaun had seen Paula at this very truck stop, arguing with a tall, dark-haired guy.

Suddenly realization dawned on her. There had to be *two* dark-haired guys involved with the exchange program. It wasn't Neil whom Shaun had seen enter the party. It was another tall, dark-haired guy.

And Nancy knew just who that person was. Now that she was sure of the blackmailer's identity, everything fell into place. Who else could have written the newsletters so they contained secret messages? Nancy thought. Who else had access to the students' records?

"But how are we going to stop him?" Nancy could hear Paula's frantic voice.

Suddenly Nancy kneeled on the seat and peered over the partition. Paula looked up, and her mouth fell open. Neil turned and flushed deep red.

"What do *you* want?" he said, scowling.

"I want to help you," Nancy said quietly. "Together we can stop Larry Taylor."

15

A Desperate Plan

Neil and Paula exchanged astonished glances. Then Neil stood up.

"I don't know what you're talking about," he said abruptly. "Come on, Paula, let's get out of here."

"I'm not going," Paula replied in a strained voice. "I'm tired of running and hiding."

Then Shaun leaned over the partition.

"Shaun!" Paula's eyes widened. "What are you doing here?"

"You can't shut me out any longer," he said gruffly. But Nancy could see tenderness in his eyes. "I want to help, too."

Paula nodded, and a tear trickled down her cheek. Nancy and Shaun walked around the tables to Paula's booth. Shaun slid next to Paula and gently took her hand. Nancy could see now that Shaun Devane had been telling the truth.

Nancy waited in the aisle to see what Neil would do. She knew she couldn't force him to accept their help.

For a moment Neil stood rigid, his face filled with indecision. Then he stepped away from the bench. "Have a seat," he said with cold politeness.

"Thanks." Nancy took off her coat, then slid across the wooden seat. "By the way, I'm Nancy Drew." She held out her hand. "We've met before, but I guess this is the first chance I've had to introduce myself." She smiled, hoping to put the Irish student at ease.

Ignoring her words, Neil sat next to Nancy, his legs stretched into the aisle as if he were ready to flee. "I know who you are," he said curtly.

The waitress came up then. "You three wanna order?" she asked. Then she glanced at Paula's untouched hamburger. "I don't blame you for not eating it, dearie. Fred's burgers are like rubber. How about something else?"

Paula pushed her plate away. "No, thanks."

"Tea sounds good to me," Nancy said.

"And I'll have a soda," Shaun said, his gaze still on Paula.

"Nothing for me," Neil muttered. He was glaring at Nancy, distrust flashing in his green eyes.

"Neil, Nancy's a detective," Paula said quietly when the waitress left. "We have to trust *someone*."

"No, we don't," he said through clenched teeth. "We agreed to handle this ourselves."

"I don't think that's a wise idea," Nancy broke in.

127

"Larry Taylor is a very clever criminal. He'll do anything to get what he wants."

"He pushed Nancy onto the lake at Le Café," Shaun said in a grave voice. "And the ice cracked beneath her."

"He could have killed you," Paula gasped.

"We don't know for sure it was him." Frowning, Nancy turned toward Neil. "Where did you go after I saw you at the restaurant?"

Neil shrugged. "I ran down to the lake, and then— Hey!" Neil noticed Nancy's suspicious expression. "You don't think *I* pushed you onto the ice?"

"Well, did you?" Shaun leaned threateningly across the table.

"No way," Neil said angrily. "I doubled back and got into my car. I was trying to find Paula. We were both running scared from Taylor."

"I believe you," Nancy said.

"What should we do?" Paula asked in a worried voice.

"First you have to tell me everything," Nancy said.

"No way," Neil blurted out again. He was nervously twirling a knife on the table. Since he wasn't the blackmailer, Nancy wondered what he had to hide.

"She's right, Neil." Paula's voice was firmer. "If we want to get Taylor, we're going to need help."

With a determined expression, she faced Nancy. "Larry Taylor is blackmailing both of us," she began. "At first he just wanted money. Then he started demanding that we do certain things for him."

"He knew about your shoplifting record," Nancy said.

Paula looked surprised, then embarrassed. "How did you find out about that? I had it hidden—"

"In your boot," Nancy finished. "But look, you were arrested when you were very young. Why were you frightened of Taylor exposing you?"

Paula stared at the table. "Well, at first I was worried about what people would think. I thought the Moorelys would be shocked and send me right home. Then after I knew everyone better and realized they'd probably understand, Taylor said he'd arrange a shoplifting incident at the boutique and make it look like I did it."

"Is that what happened the day we met?" Nancy asked.

Paula shook her head. "No. That night I was supposed to unlock the jewelry case, then turn the other way when Babette came into the store. She's another exchange student Larry was using."

"Only you couldn't go through with it," Nancy guessed.

Paula nodded. "Everyone at the boutique has been so good to me. But then Ms. Hunt unlocked the case to show a necklace to a customer."

"So when Babette stole the jewelry, you decided to catch her."

Paula chuckled. "Larry was furious! He was the

129

one who knocked me down in the alley outside the post office. He said if I didn't shape up, I might not live to regret it."

Shaun smacked his fist on the table. "That creep. Wait'll I get my hands on him!"

"I told him he couldn't make me steal from the boutique," Paula said defiantly.

"Until he threatened the Moorelys," Nancy said.

Paula nodded, then cast her eyes at Neil.

"All right. I'll tell her," he said at last. He turned in the booth to face Nancy, his green eyes flashing with anger. "Taylor was using me as the middle-man. I collected the money and sent Paula the messages, but that's all."

Nancy didn't think so.

Judging from his accent, he'd obviously made the call to the Moorelys' house. And Nancy remembered the look of terror on his face when she'd spoken to him at the fire. Had he been the one who had lit the gas-soaked rags in the basement?

Nancy decided to confront him directly. "So if you didn't work for Larry, he was going to set a fire, then accuse you. Right?"

Neil flushed. "He'd found out somehow that I was once suspected of arson back in Ireland. But I had nothing to do with the fire at the Moorelys'. You've got to believe me!"

"Then why did I see you there that night?" Nancy asked.

Neil shrugged. "Taylor sent me to Paula's house on a wild-goose chase. I had no idea until I saw the fire trucks that there'd been a fire. Then I realized he'd set it up so I'd be placed at the scene of the crime. That's why I panicked when you saw me."

Suddenly, Nancy remembered something Larry Taylor had said when he'd stopped by her house.

"I believe you," Nancy said slowly. "And I think I can prove Taylor set you up. He made one slip when I met him earlier this evening. He told me he'd recognize the Moorelys' bright yellow house. He also mentioned that he hadn't been there since August. Well, in August, the house was gray."

"That's right!" Paula gasped. "So unless he'd been there—"

"The night of the fire," Neil finished her sentence, "there's no way he could have known the new color was yellow." With a look of relief, he reached over and thumped Nancy on the back. "You may just have saved my life."

Nancy grinned at the Irish student's obvious relief. "Don't get too excited yet. I'm afraid we need more on Larry Taylor than that. Paula, tell me what's supposed to happen on Saturday."

Paula's eyes widened in shock. "How did you know about Saturday?"

"I found a few of those newsletters in your room."

"But how did you figure out the code?" Paula asked.

Nancy laughed. "I'm a detective, remember?"

"Right." The Dutch girl chuckled. Nancy was glad to see she was finally beginning to relax. Paula had been under tremendous pressure the last few months.

131

"Okay," Paula went on. "Here's the story. To-morrow the boutique is getting a shipment of gold and diamond jewelry from Africa. Before it's all accounted for, Larry wants me to put a box of it away. I'm supposed to meet him later in the under-ground parking lot and give the box to him."

"Only she doesn't want to do it," Neil said.

"Here's your order, dearies." Paula jumped ner-vously as the waitress plopped a teacup and a glass on the table.

Nancy waited until the waitress had scribbled their check and walked away. "Did Larry say he'd make sure you got all the blame if you didn't do it?" Nancy asked finally.

Paula smiled nervously. "Worse than that." She glanced up at Shaun. "He said he'd make it look like Shaun was my partner."

"What?" Shaun asked in surprise. "How does he know about me?"

"Not only does he know about you," Paula said, "but when I met him here Monday night, he told me about your prior police record."

Shaun whistled. "I have to hand it to this Taylor guy. He really sets things up carefully. I was ar-rested for breaking and entering last year," he explained to Nancy. "It was a stupid prank. Fortu-nately, since I was a juvenile, they let me off easy. I've been clean ever since. But it sure would be easy to make me look like a guilty partner."

Nancy nodded gravely. "That proves Larry Taylor's even more ruthless than I thought. To catch him, we're going to need a foolproof plan."

132

She'd have to contact the police and let them know Paula was okay. She'd also need to get some help nailing Larry Taylor. But first she had to figure out a way to catch him.

Then Nancy's gaze focused on Paula's heavy parka hanging over the back of the booth. Sticking out of the pocket was a stocking cap.

"Excuse me," she said to Neil.

When he stood up, she slid out. "May I borrow these a minute?" she asked Paula, pointing toward the Dutch girl's coat and cap.

"Sure," Paula answered in a puzzled voice.

Nancy draped the coat over her arm and headed to the rest room. Five minutes later, she walked back down the aisle wearing Paula's parka. Her hair was tucked into the hat, and the coat collar was buttoned high around her neck.

She stopped at the table and swung Paula's white leather bag over her shoulder.

"Well? How do I look?" she asked the others.

"Like me," Paula said. "All you need is a braid down your back."

"And your boots and gloves," Nancy added. "The lights in the underground parking lot are pretty dim, I think. If I don't get too close to him, Taylor won't know it's me."

"Are you going to take Taylor the jewels from the boutique?" Neil asked.

"I'll take him jewels, all right, but they won't be from the boutique. We'll have to find substitutes that'll fool him long enough for the police to catch him in the act."

133

Nancy looked at Paula. "Were you supposed to contact Taylor tonight?"

"Yes," Paula answered. "At the party. He was going to give me the time and exact spot to meet him on Saturday."

"It might not be too late," Nancy said. "Let's call Le Café and see if he's still there."

The girls found a phone booth at the back of the diner. Nancy looked up the number, and Paula dialed. Nancy watched as she wrote down the information.

"All right, Larry. Nine o'clock. First tier of the parking lot," Paula repeated in a cool voice. "I'll look for a blue station wagon in the third row of cars. Don't worry. You can count on me this time."

Good work, Paula, Nancy thought. But when the blond girl hung up the phone, her face was pale, and all its eagerness had been erased.

Nancy touched her shoulder. "What's wrong?"

Paula swallowed. "He said if he even sees a policeman, I'll never be able to sleep again. If I mess up this time, he'll set the Moorelys' whole house on fire, with all of them in it!"

16

No Way Out

"Don't worry," Nancy said to Paula. "We'll call the Moorelys right now and warn them."

"You're not going to call the police, are you?" Paula asked Nancy.

"We have to," Nancy stated firmly.

"But Larry said he'd burn the Moorelys' house down if he saw any police," Paula said, grabbing hold of Nancy's sleeve.

"We'll have the police patrol the Moorelys' street, too, and watch the house. And we'll make sure no one's home until Taylor is caught."

Paula looked desperately into Nancy's eyes. "Maybe that will be enough. What should we do next?"

"We have to explain to your boss, Ms. Hunt, what our plan is so she knows what to expect tomorrow. Then we'll ask Bess if we can borrow some of her jewelry to use instead of the real jewelry."

Paula sighed shakily and said, "I hope this works."

"You're not meeting Taylor without backup," Shaun said. "So you need to include us."

"And Paula should coach you on your accent," Neil warned.

"Okay." Nancy shrugged. "So the plan has some wrinkles we need to iron out. But everyone agrees we get Taylor, right?" She looked from face to face.

"Right!" the others chorused eagerly.

"That braid really makes you look like Paula," Bess said. She and Nancy were waiting with Suzanne by the fountain at the mall. It was eight-fifteen on Saturday night. The girls were meeting Shaun to discuss final plans.

"Let's just hope Larry Taylor thinks so," Nancy replied. She was dressed in the outfit that Paula had worn when she'd first met Taylor at the truck stop. Fortunately, Nancy and the exchange student were about the same size, although Paula was slightly taller.

"I don't see him anywhere." Suzanne glanced around the crowded walkways.

"I'm right here," a deep voice said.

The three girls twirled in surprise. Shaun was standing behind Bess, dressed in coveralls and a cap. He was pulling a trash can that had a dust pan, a broom, and bottles of cleaning solutions attached to it. But what amazed Nancy most was that his hair had been cut short.

"Is that really you?" Suzanne gasped.

"Wow." Nancy laughed. "Taylor's never going to suspect it's you."

"That's the idea, isn't it?" Shaun grinned. "I borrowed this outfit from a friend. I want to make sure Larry Taylor doesn't get away." He nodded toward Bess and Suzanne. "Actually, it took me a minute to recognize you two."

Bess beamed. She and Suzanne had worked hard on their disguises as stylish shoppers. Even though Taylor had never seen Bess, she still wanted to look the part.

Both girls wore plenty of makeup and wigs that were darker than their hair colors. They were also wearing high heels and fancy dresses. Loaded with armfuls of bags and packages, they hoped to pass for two socialites out shopping.

"Okay, let's synchronize our watches." Nancy glanced at hers. "It's now eight-twenty. At eight-forty, I'll leave Around the World and head for the parking lot. I'll take the elevator. Shaun, you'll already be on tier one emptying the trash cans."

She turned to Bess and Suzanne. "At nine o'clock on the dot, you two come down the steps to tier one. Pass right by the blue station wagon. Remember, all three of you have to be witnesses to Taylor taking the jewels."

"Where will the police be stationed?" Bess asked nervously.

"They'll be watching the outside entrances to the garage in case Taylor gets away," Nancy told her. "Also, two plainclothes cops will be on tier one. Chief McGinnis didn't say how they'd be disguised.

He was afraid someone might blow their covers by accident. If Taylor gets suspicious, he might get dangerous. Remember what he said about starting another fire."

"Right," Suzanne said solemnly. "It's a good thing my parents are staying with our neighbors and the police are watching our house." Then she grimaced. "That guy had both my parents fooled last night when he stopped by. They thought he was so concerned about Paula, but the whole time he was pumping them for information that would help him find her."

"He's clever, all right. So let's watch out." Nancy took a deep breath. "Are we ready?"

The others nodded.

"Then let's go," Nancy said.

Shaun wheeled his cart away and began to pick up trash. Bess and Suzanne, acting as if they were deep in conversation, strolled down the walkway.

Nancy watched them leave, her heart pounding. She went up the escalator to Around the World. As soon as Paula saw Nancy, she stepped out the back door, leaving her bag and parka. She was going to meet Neil outside. The two of them would be in Chief McGinnis's patrol car, helping to watch for Taylor.

Nancy waved to Ms. Hunt. The manager gave her a secret wink, then turned back to a customer. Nancy began to straighten some merchandise on a shelf. If Taylor had spies watching the store, she wanted things to look as normal as possible.

At eight-forty, Nancy told Ms. Hunt that she had

a headache and needed to go home. After glancing in Paula's leather bag to make sure the box of jewelry was there, she slipped on the heavy parka and headed out the front entrance of the boutique.

Inside the box were several pieces of costume jewelry that Bess had donated for the night. Paula had placed the necklaces, rings, and bracelets in a small shipping carton that was identical to the ones that had just arrived. Nancy hoped they would fool Taylor for a short while, at least.

Outside the boutique, Nancy paused to pull on her stocking cap and turn up her coat collar. Then she walked quickly to the elevator and pressed the down button.

The elevator stopped, and Nancy stepped inside. But before she could turn, someone grabbed her arm from behind.

"There's been a change of plans," a hoarse voice whispered in her ear as the doors closed behind them. "Press the button for tier two."

Nancy froze. Strong fingers squeezed her arm through the coat, and a blunt object pressed into her back.

It has to be Taylor, her racing mind told her. And he has a gun!

Nancy turned slowly toward the doors. Taylor stuck close behind her. Keeping her face turned carefully away from him, she raised her hand to press the button for tier two, then hesitated. If it was Taylor and he'd already seen her face, she didn't dare get off.

But if he thought she was Paula, she still had a

chance to carry out the plan. It would be riskier, but the police could still catch him leaving the parking lot with the "stolen" goods.

"Do it, Paula," the voice commanded. Then he chuckled nastily. "You must have known I wouldn't trust you and your meddling friends."

He thinks I'm Paula, Nancy realized. With shaking fingers, she reached up and pressed the button.

The elevator doors opened on tier two, and the empty parking lot loomed in front of Nancy. Her stomach tightened in a knot.

"Let's go," Taylor hissed as he jabbed Nancy with the gun. "Over to the green sedan."

Nancy's heart fell to her knees with a clunk. The police were on the lookout for a blue station wagon. That meant Taylor had driven into the parking lot undetected. Nancy could only hope that Neil or Paula would still spot him.

Or maybe the police and her friends on the bottom tier would get suspicious when she didn't show up. Nancy checked her watch. Eight-forty-five. They weren't expecting her until nine o'clock. She'd have to stall Taylor.

"Come on," he urged. "If you do as I say, you won't get hurt."

He pushed Nancy from behind. Crying out convincingly, she stumbled forward. Nancy wanted him to think she'd been frightened into silence. It wasn't too hard to fake.

Quickly, Nancy wound her way through the cars to the green sedan.

"Now, hand me the box," Taylor ordered.

Keeping her head bowed, Nancy reached into the leather bag. Taylor grabbed the box, tore the taped seal, and pulled out a gold necklace.

"Ah-h-h-h." He held it up to the light and twirled it around. Slowly, Nancy inched away from him. If she could just get behind the car, maybe she could make a run for it.

Suddenly, Taylor's face clouded, and he threw the necklace to the ground. "This is a fake!" he cried, lunging for her.

Spinning on her heels, Nancy tried to run, but Taylor grabbed her coat sleeve and swung her around like a top. He grabbed her stocking cap along with the coat, and the hat flew off her head.

"Why, you sneaky little traitor," he sneered. "What made you think you could get away—" Suddenly, he caught sight of Nancy's face. For a long moment, he stared at her. Then his eyes narrowed. "So we meet again, Miss Drew."

"Let me go, Taylor." Nancy struggled against the tall man's grasp, but he only clamped down tighter on her arm. "The police will be here any second," she told him.

"Fine." Taylor opened the front door of the car and threw Nancy in roughly. "You'll be my ticket out of here."

Nancy scrambled over the gearshift and into the passenger seat. Taylor climbed in, the gun aimed at her.

"And don't try anything funny," he added as he started the motor.

When he turned his head to back up, Nancy

sneaked her hand over to the passenger door and flipped up the lock. If only she could distract him long enough to jump out.

Taylor threw the car into forward. His gun was in the hand that held the steering wheel. As Taylor maneuvered the car, the gun rotated dangerously in all directions.

Stepping on the gas, Taylor headed for the ramp that would lead him up and out of the parking lot. The speedometer hit thirty as he careened around a row of cars.

Nancy grabbed the door handle, trying to keep her balance. If she didn't get out before he reached the street, she might never get the chance!

Suddenly, a flash of white caught her eye. She glanced in her side mirror. A car was zooming up behind them. Nancy's mouth fell open. It was Shaun's old car. She could see him hunched over the steering wheel, his cap tilted back on his head.

Taylor glanced in his rearview mirror. Cursing under his breath, he took a sharp left.

"You and your little playmates must think you're a match for me." He grinned maliciously. "Too bad I'll have to prove you all wrong."

Nancy glared at him. "Since you haven't gotten away with anything, I'd say we were *more* than a match."

He laughed. "Haven't gotten away? Just watch me." He nodded toward the exit ramp. "In another minute, I'll be home free."

Frantically, Nancy looked out the back window. Where was Shaun?

The sedan zipped toward the last ~~braked~~, and Nancy saw her chance. She pun~~ched~~ the door handle. When the door swung wide, she covered her head with her arms. Then, shoulder first, she propelled herself from the car.

Nancy hit the concrete floor with a thud and rolled away from the tires. The heavy parka cushioned her fall. Quickly, she scrambled to her feet, prepared to run.

But Taylor wasn't interested in stopping to chase her. With a squeal of brakes, he turned and started up the exit ramp.

Then she heard a long, loud honk. Speeding the wrong way down the ramp, heading straight for Taylor's car, was Shaun Devane.

Nancy clapped her hand over her mouth. There was no way either driver could stop in time. They were going to crash!

17

Unpaid Crimes

Nancy gave a shout and ran toward the ramp, waving her arms. Then she glimpsed Shaun through the front windshield. He was glaring at the other car, his face frozen in a determined frown. He knew Taylor was coming right for him, and he wasn't slowing down.

The two cars drew closer and closer. Nancy stifled a scream. At the last minute, Taylor's car swerved sharply and crashed into a support pole.

The old white car zoomed down the ramp and braked next to Nancy. Shaun jumped out. "Are you all right?" he asked anxiously.

"Fine," she said. "Except you scared me to death. I thought you guys were going to crash. Come on, we'd better check Taylor."

The two of them rushed over to the green car.

Larry Taylor was slumped over the steering wheel, moaning. Nancy could hear sirens in the background.

"We'll have to call an ambulance," Nancy said.

"The police are coming," Shaun replied. "They'll call."

"How much do the police know?" Nancy asked.

"When you didn't show up at nine o'clock, we figured something went wrong. The undercover cops went up to Around the World to follow your trail. On a hunch, I jumped in my car and headed down here."

"Good thinking," Nancy said. "But how did you get on the ramp to head us off? You were behind us, right? Then you were ahead of us!"

"Did I ever tell you I used to drive in a demolition derby?" Shaun grinned.

The sirens drew closer, and two patrol cars roared down the ramp. One of them stopped next to Shaun's car, and Officer Brody stepped out.

"Just couldn't wait for backup, huh, Ms. Drew?" he greeted her.

She laughed. "Well, this wasn't exactly how it was supposed to turn out. But at least we got Taylor." She pointed to the car. Brody's partner was opening the door.

"Yeah. We got our man." After telling his partner to call an ambulance, Brody pulled out his notebook. "And I got that insurance information you wanted," he said to Nancy. "There's no way the Moorelys could have torched their own place."

Nancy had to laugh. "Gee, thanks, Officer. That's just what I needed to wrap this case up."

"Chicken?" Paula repeated, looking puzzled. "I thought that was a bird."

"Explain what playing chicken is to Neil and Paula," Nancy said to Shaun. "That's what really did Larry Taylor in."

It was Sunday afternoon, and everyone connected to the Taylor case was in the private room of Le Café. They were having a celebration now that Taylor had been caught.

Nancy's dad and Mr. and Mrs. Moorely were talking at another table.

"When you play chicken," Shaun began, "two cars and their drivers face each other on a road, and they zoom toward each other."

"Just like you and Taylor did on the ramp," Bess added.

Shaun nodded. "Right. And the first person to swerve out of the way is the chicken."

Paula gasped. "But that's crazy. What if no one swerves?"

Shaun shrugged. "Then you crash. But usually that doesn't happen. Someone always loses his nerve."

"Like Taylor did," Nancy said.

"You must be the best chicken player in River Heights," Bess exclaimed.

Shaun grinned. "Nah. Only last year, when I was young and wild."

Suzanne turned to Nancy. "I'm so mad I missed
146

out on all the excitement." She slapped the table angrily.

"Excitement? My heart still hasn't slowed down." Nancy laughed. "We should have guessed Taylor had an alternate plan so Paula couldn't double-cross him."

"He knew everything else," Neil reminded her. "Like all our police records."

"I can explain that," Nancy told him. "It seems Mr. Taylor's brother is a detective in Chicago. He was in on all of this, too, I guess. Anyway, all Taylor had to do was supply a name, and this brother could get any info he wanted. He even had connections abroad."

"And once Taylor had the information, he used it to blackmail certain students," Paula said bitterly.

"And until you and Neil decided to fight back, he'd been getting away with it," Nancy said, shaking her head. "The other kids were too scared. Taylor always knew exactly what to threaten them with."

Paula nodded. "He knew I didn't want the Moorelys hurt."

"And he told me I'd be shipped straight back to Ireland," Neil added.

Carson Drew came up to stand behind Nancy. "Well, kids, I've just discussed things with the Moorelys, and I've talked to Neil's and Paula's parents. Everyone agrees it would be best if you both testified against Taylor."

"Great," Neil said vehemently. "I want to see him behind bars."

"We can get Taylor on both blackmail and kidnapping." Mr. Drew smiled at his daughter. "I don't think he realized what a big mistake he made when he forced you into the car, Nancy."

"What about stealing?" Paula asked.

Mr. Drew shook his head. "That's too hard to prove, I'm afraid. But I did track down the French student, Babette. She's willing to testify that Taylor forced her to shoplift."

"Can they prove he started the fire at the Moorelys'?" Neil asked.

"We think so," Mr. Drew replied. "Officer Brody's been on that case. The police searched Taylor's car and found traces of fibers from the rags used to set the fire. There were drops of spilled gas in his trunk as well."

"Whew!" Neil breathed a sigh of relief.

"So Taylor's in big trouble," Nancy said.

Her dad nodded. "Especially since Neil, Paula, and Babette are under eighteen and considered minors."

"I'd like to thank everyone." Paula looked apologetically at all of the friends surrounding her. "Neil and I should have trusted you all in the first place."

"That's right!" Suzanne put her hands on her hips. "Then Nancy and I could have cracked this case ages ago."

Everyone laughed.

"Well, Detective Moorely," Bess said to Suzanne. "Why don't you solve the Case of the Missing Jewels for me?"

"What missing jewels?" Suzanne asked.

148

"*My* jewels. The ones you promised to return after Taylor was caught. They may not have been precious diamonds, but they're all I've got."

"Oh, right." Suzanne looked flustered. "Let's see. They were last seen clutched in Larry Taylor's hand." She snapped her fingers. "That must mean he's still got them."

Bess groaned. "I knew I'd never see them again."

Nancy laughed. "Don't worry, Bess. I rescued your jewelry before the police arrived. I knew they'd take them as evidence if I didn't."

"So where are they?"

Nancy pretended to think. "The clues tell me they're in a pocket of a red—no, blue—coat."

Bess reached around and pulled her coat off the back of her chair. "I have a blue coat." She stuck her hand in her pocket and pulled out a small box. Tucked safely inside were all her necklaces, bracelets, and rings.

"Case closed," Bess said with a grin.

"Well, Nancy Drew," Paula said, "*dank u*— again. You are a great detective!"

NANCY DREW® MYSTERY STORIES By Carolyn Keene

☐ THE TRIPLE HOAX—#57
69153 $3.50

☐ THE FLYING SAUCER MYSTERY—#58
72320 $3.50

☐ THE SECRET IN THE OLD LACE—#59
69067 $3.99

☐ THE GREEK SYMBOL MYSTERY—#60
67457 $3.50

☐ THE SWAMI'S RING—#61
62467 $3.50

☐ THE KACHINA DOLL MYSTERY—#62
67220 $3.50

☐ THE TWIN DILEMMA—#63
67301 $3.50

☐ CAPTIVE WITNESS—#64
70471 $3.50

☐ MYSTERY OF THE WINGED LION—#65
62681 $3.50

☐ RACE AGAINST TIME—#66
69485 $3.50

☐ THE SINISTER OMEN—#67
73938 $3.50

☐ THE ELUSIVE HEIRESS—#68
62478 $3.99

☐ CLUE IN THE ANCIENT DISGUISE—#69
64279 $3.50

☐ THE BROKEN ANCHOR—#70
62481 $3.50

☐ THE SILVER COBWEB—#71
70992 $3.50

☐ THE HAUNTED CAROUSEL—#72
66227 $3.50

☐ ENEMY MATCH—#73
64283 $3.50

☐ MYSTERIOUS IMAGE—#74
69401 $3.50

☐ THE EMERALD-EYED CAT MYSTERY—#75
64282 $3.50

☐ THE ESKIMO'S SECRET—#76
73003 $3.50

☐ THE BLUEBEARD ROOM—#77
66857 $3.50

☐ THE PHANTOM OF VENICE—#78
73422 $3.50

☐ THE DOUBLE HORROR
OF FENLEY PLACE—#79
64387 $3.50

☐ THE CASE OF THE DISAPPEARING
DIAMONDS—#80
64896 $3.50

☐ MARDI GRAS MYSTERY—#81
64961 $3.50

☐ THE CLUE IN THE CAMERA—#82
64962 $3.50

☐ THE CASE OF THE VANISHING VEIL—#83
63413 $3.50

☐ THE JOKER'S REVENGE—#84
63414 $3.50

☐ THE SECRET OF SHADY GLEN—#85
63416 $3.50

☐ THE MYSTERY OF MISTY CANYON—#86
63417 $3.99

☐ THE CASE OF THE RISING STARS—#87
66312 $3.50

☐ THE SEARCH FOR CINDY AUSTIN—#88
66313 $3.50

☐ THE CASE OF THE DISAPPEARING DEEJAY—#89
66314 $3.50

☐ THE PUZZLE AT PINEVIEW SCHOOL—#90
66315 $3.95

☐ THE GIRL WHO COULDN'T REMEMBER—#91
66316 $3.50

☐ THE GHOST OF CRAVEN COVE—#92
66317 $3.50

☐ THE CASE OF
THE SAFECRACKER'S SECRET—#93
66318 $3.50

☐ THE PICTURE PERFECT MYSTERY—#94
66315 $3.50

☐ THE SILENT SUSPECT—#95
69280 $3.50

☐ THE CASE OF THE PHOTO FINISH—#96
69281 $3.50

☐ THE MYSTERY AT
MAGNOLIA MANSION—#97
69282 $3.50

☐ THE HAUNTING OF HORSE ISLAND—#98
69284 $3.50

☐ THE SECRET AT SEVEN ROCKS—#99
69285 $3.50

☐ A SECRET IN TIME—#100
69286 $3.50

☐ THE MYSTERY OF THE MISSING MILLIONAIRESS—#101
69287 $3.50

☐ THE SECRET IN THE DARK—#102
69279 $3.50

☐ THE STRANGER IN THE SHADOWS—#103
73049 $3.50

☐ NANCY DREW® GHOST STORIES—#1
69132 $3.50

and don't forget...THE HARDY BOYS® Now available in paperback

---

THE HARDY BOYS® SERIES By Franklin W. Dixon